Haunted High Book 4

Cage the Beast

By Cheree Alsop

ISBN:1985590735
Cover Design by Robert Emerson
Editing by Sue Player
www.ChereeAlsop.com

To my family:
My love for you is without end.

To my readers:
May home be the place you return
At the end of every adventure.

ALSO BY CHEREE ALSOP

The Haunted High Series-

The Wolf Within Me
The Ghost Files
City of Demons
Cage the Beast
Ashes of Night

The Silver Series-

Silver
Black
Crimson
Violet
Azure
Hunter
Silver Moon

The Werewolf Academy Series-

Book One: Strays
Book Two: Hunted
Book Three: Instinct
Book Four: Taken
Book Five: Lost
Book Six: Vengeance
Book Seven: Chosen

Heart of the Wolf Part One
Heart of the Wolf Part Two

The Galdoni Series-

Galdoni
Galdoni 2: Into the Storm
Galdoni 3: Out of Darkness

The Small Town Superheroes Series-

Small Town Superhero
Small Town Superhero II
Small Town Superhero III

Keeper of the Wolves
Stolen
The Million Dollar Gift
Thief Prince
When Death Loved an Angel

The Shadows Series

Shadows- Book One in the World of Shadows
Mist- Book Two in the World of Shadows

The Monster Asylum Series

Book One- The Fangs of Bloodhaven
Book Two- The Scales of Drakenfall

Girl from the Stars

Book 1- Daybreak
Book 2- Daylight
Book 3- Day's End
Book 4- Day's Journey

Book 5- Day's Hunt

The Pirate from the Stars

The Dr. Wolf Series

Book 1- Shockwave
Book 2- Demon Spiral
Book 3- The Four Horsemen
Book 4- Dragon's Bayne

The Prince of Ash and Blood

Chapter One

I STARED AT THE message on my cellphone until the words blurred together and no longer made sense. For a week, there had been peace. The Mythic Labs had been shut down, the two pieces of Chutka the Shambler's heart were confined in separate ironwood boxes and hidden where only Mercer and Professor Briggs knew, and nobody had mentioned demons for at least five days. I had actually started to feel like a normal student at The Remus Academy for Integral Education, and that was saying something. All of that was shattered by the text from my brother.

GRAYSON NEWTON TOOK MOM AND DAD. HE SAID HE WILL RANSOM THEM FOR YOUR VAMPIRE SO HE CAN GET INTO SOMETHING CALLED THE MASS. HELP ME FINN!!- DRAKE

Grayson wanted Vicken so he could prove to the Monster Abolition and Eradication Society that he belonged with them. Grayson's brother Sebastian had died in a car accident the same night that I found out I was a werewolf. Because of me, Grayson believed the monster rumors, and the chip he carried on his shoulder from his brother's death had somehow turned into a vendetta, not just against me, but against every monster. Now Dad and Julianne were involved. Sending me to Haunted High hadn't protected any of us the way we had hoped it would. With Julianne nearly nine months pregnant, time was also a luxury I couldn't afford.

I opened the door of the room Alden and I shared and was about to head downstairs when a hand touched my arm.

"Where are you off to?"

Dara had an uncanny ability of finding me whenever something was wrong. I felt her pull and knew the empath could read the anxiety and fear the text had invoked. I opened my mouth, but couldn't speak. Wordlessly, I held out the cellphone. She mouthed the words of the text and then looked up at me, her violet eyes wide.

"Is this for real?"

I nodded. "I've got to go find out what Drake knows. But first—"

"First you need to talk to Vicken," she completed. "He's probably at lunch. I'll go find him and send him up here."

Gratitude for the empath's understanding filled me. "Thank you," I told her.

She hurried to the stairs and then paused. "But you're not going without me."

I stared at her. "Dara, he said Grayson's in touch with the Maes. There's no way I'm letting you get involved."

"And there's no way I'm letting you go without coming with you. I'm tired of being told to stay behind while you put yourself in danger. I'm already involved, Finn. Accept it." She turned, her ashen hair swishing across her back as she ran down the stairs.

I don't know what she said to my friends, but the speed with which they returned surprised me.

"We're going," Vicken said before I could say a word. "I'll grab my coat."

The vampire shoved past me to head up the stairs. Dara followed him.

"Of course we're going," Alden said. The little Grim tried to step around me into our room.

I caught him arm.

"I need you to stay here."

The Grim stared at me. "What are you talking about? We're a team, remember?"

I shook my head. "Alden, you almost died at the Mythic Labs. If those scientists had been using bullets instead of tranquilizers, you would've been a name on your mom or dad's arm. I can't ask you to do that again."

Alden's mouth opened, closed, and then opened again and he said, "But we're a team."

I could hear the hurt in his voice. He was right. He had been at my side on every dangerous adventure from fighting demons to freeing mythics. I couldn't imagine going without him, but my instincts warned that he needed to stay. Somewhere along the line, I had learned to trust my instincts.

I gestured for him to go into our room and followed him inside. I sat on the edge of my bed. He did the same on his so that we faced each other.

"Alden, you were my first friend here."

"You're only friend," the Grim reminded me.

I nodded. "My only friend. You weren't afraid of the fact that I'm a werewolf, and your acceptance helped others give me a chance."

Alden nodded without speaking. His head was lowered so that his eyes were shielded by his white hair. I felt bad for the dejected slope of his shoulders and the way he didn't want to look at me.

I let out a steadying breath and said, "When that demon took over your body and I went hunting for you in the Otherworld, I was so afraid I wouldn't find you. And then when that scientist shot you at the Labs, I was afraid you'd been killed. I almost killed them," I admitted. I remembered pointing the gun at their unconscious forms, ready to end their lives for hurting my friend. My voice lowered. "If it wasn't for Vicken, I would have, and that scares me more than anything."

"Why?" Alden's voice was quiet when he looked up at me.

I replied with full honesty, "Because if someone hurts any of my friends, I'm not sure I can control my wolf side enough not to seek revenge." I opened and closed my right hand, looking detachedly at the burn that refused to heal on my palm. "Something comes over me, and it's like I'm full animal, ready to do anything to protect those I care about. It's a bit scary."

"So if you're worried, why is Dara going with you?"

I felt my cheeks redden at the intensity of his scrutiny. I knew I owed him a full explanation, but I didn't quite know it myself. I went with, "Because I can control my wolf side better when I'm around her."

The Grim gave a little, reluctant nod. "That makes sense seeing how she's an empath. But what about Vicken?"

"If I lose control, I can't really hurt him that bad," I replied.

"But you could hurt me," Alden said.

My heart clenched at the expression on the little Grim's face. He was so pale and skinny. I had no doubt I could snap him like a twig if I was at my full werewolf strength. It would have been an easy way out of the conversation, but I shook my head. "I would never hurt you. I just can't be responsible if something happens on my watch. I don't think I could control myself then."

Alden nodded. "Because of Sebastian."

The name of Grayson's brother who had died in the river accident made me cringe inwardly. I hadn't thought about it in those terms, but I had to admit that the Grim was right. "Yeah," I said quietly. "I can't lose another friend like that."

"What about Sparrow?"

I lifted my wrist to look at the sleeping sylph dragon. Her black and purple scales lifted and fell with each steady breath. The dragon's wings were pulled tight along her body and her claws rested gently against my skin.

"What about her?" I asked.

"She almost died, too," Alden pressed. "Actually, she did die, but she chose to come back and I heard you promise her that you wouldn't put her in any more danger." He rushed on to say, "You left her with Dara last time. Can I watch her if I stay?"

A smile touched my lips. "That would be great! I don't dare take her where we're going and she already knows you. That would really help me out." I ran a finger down Sparrow's back and said, "Sparrow, wake up sleepyhead."

The dragon raised her head and blinked her bright green eyes. I couldn't help smiling when her forked red tongue ran across her muzzle. "I've got to go somewhere for a few days," I told her. "I need you to stay with Alden. He'll keep you safe and make sure you eat."

Alden rose and crossed eagerly to me. "I've always wondered what it would be like to have a pet dragon. Do you think she'll be okay with me?"

Sparrow unwrapped from my wrist and crossed to my palm. She shook herself, ending in a swish of her long purple and black tail.

"I'll think she'll do great," I reassured him. "She looks hungry. Do you want to take her hunting for bugs? We usually find a few up on the thirteenth floor."

"Awesome," Alden replied. He lifted his hand next to mine.

Sparrow crossed to it, then hesitated and looked at me. I nodded encouragingly. "I won't be gone long, I promise," I reassured her. "And Alden will make sure you get lots of food." I brought her closer and said, "Trust me, he knows the good stuff."

"Does she like burritos?" he asked. I could feel him practically buzzing with excitement when she stepped onto his palm.

"I know she likes spaghetti and eggs. She hasn't tried much else. Just make sure she has a few bugs every day to balance out her diet."

He nodded quickly, his smile wide at the dragon's attention. "We'll find plenty of bugs. And I'll bet she likes hot dogs. Oh, and she should try bacon. I've heard dragons like bacon." Sparrow tipped her head at his words as though she was trying to understand. It made him laugh. He shot me another smile. "Also, ice cream. I'll bet I can convince Mr. Handsworth to donate some from the cafeteria for such a worthy cause."

"If anyone can convince him, you can," I replied.

Alden walked out of the door still talking. "French fries are the best, oh, and taquitos. I wonder if dragons like taquitos. And tacos. We should definitely try tacos…."

His voice faded as he went down the stairs. My heart gave a little pang of regret at the dragon's absence. My left wrist tingled. I turned it over to see Sparrow's name written in gray lettering there. It felt strange not to have the dragon sleeping over the scrolled word.

"Ready to go?" Dara asked from the doorway.

Vicken waited silently behind her. His long black trench coat and his long black hair he kept pulled back in a ponytail made him look like an intimidating wraith. I was grateful he was on our side.

I tried to appear more certain than I felt when I nodded. "Ready."

I grabbed my coat from the hook on the wall and as about to leave when a thought hit me. I hurriedly slipped out of the shoes I was wearing and pulled on a ratty pair from the closet instead.

At Dara's questioning look, I explained, "I've lost enough shoes from phasing to wolf form. The least I can do is leave the shoes I don't want to lose."

She nodded. "That's something I never thought about. How about your shirt?"

I glanced back at her as we hurried down the stairs. "I don't care about my shirt as much as my shoes."

"Isn't one item of clothing as important as the next?" Vicken asked with confusion in his voice.

I shook my head. "I used to run track at my last school. Believe me when I say a good pair of shoes can make all the difference."

"Of course," Vicken replied. "That's why you're always running toward danger. It's the running you like, not the danger."

"He always runs toward danger?" Dara asked from behind me as I pulled open the main door.

"Always," Vicken replied. "It's a nasty habit of his that I'm trying to break."

I rolled my eyes. "Can you stop talking about me like I'm not here?"

"If you keep running toward danger, you might not be," Vicken pointed out.

Dara shut the door behind us. "I agree with Vicken," she said as she followed us down the stairs.

I let out a breath. "I'm not always running toward danger."

"You ran toward the demon-possessed mountain lions," Vicken pointed out.

"I was there," Dara seconded. "You ran toward them."

"To save your lives," I replied shortly.

"How about running with a horde of demons behind you into a tiny room that would have been your chamber of death if it hadn't been for this amazing vampire I know?" Vicken asked with a pleased look on his face.

"You're the one who got bit," I said. "I was fine."

"That's beside the point," he replied. "What about chasing Lark? You ran right to the bridge and jumped off after her."

I barely blinked when the iron gate in the alley swung out to let us pass.

"She would have died if I didn't jump," I reminded the vampire.

"Just the same, I think it says something about a person who runs toward danger instead of away. Dara, don't you think that's a sigh of insanity?" Vicken questioned.

"I do, but do you know what else is insane?" Dara shot back. "Ordering a limo to take us to Finn's hometown. That's a little much, Vicken. I thought we were supposed to be keeping a low profile."

I looked up from where I had been glaring at the ground and realized that a long white limo was indeed waiting for us in front of the Pizza Palace. I wondered if the occupants inside the pizza restaurant were hopeful about some celebrity visiting their humble store.

"We're keeping a low profile," Vicken replied. "I'd just prefer not to spend my entire day in a bus. The last one was poorly driven, occupied by all manner of miscreants, and frankly, it smelled." He gestured toward the limo. "We can avoid all of that and I'll have the driver drop us off at whatever inconspicuous location Finn decides."

We slept in the limo and awoke to find ourselves entering Cleary just after sunrise. But doing so inconspicuously wasn't the right word. Students were heading to school and as we passed, they nudged each other and stared. I couldn't remember ever seeing a limousine in town when I was growing up. It would be the talk of Cleary. I had planned on having the driver stop at the grocery store near my neighborhood, but by the amount of stares the limo got just driving down Main Street, I changed my mind.

"We need to turn back. The driver can let us off at the edge of town."

"Why?" Vicken protested. "We're keeping a low profile."

"If low profile means drawing the interest of everyone in this place, then we're doing a great job," Dara replied drily.

It was clear by the vampire's expression that he wasn't used to considering situations from someone else's point of view.

I went with a different tactic. "The goal is to sneak up on Grayson, right? If everyone's attention is on the limo, maybe we can use it to distract him, too."

Dara caught on. "We can get dropped off at the edge of town and then your driver can swing back and make a few passes along the main street. That'd be a great diversion."

Vicken nodded, but he didn't look happy about the plan. "Seems like a waste of perfectly good transportation to me," he muttered. But he informed the driver of the change.

I breathed a sigh of relief when we stepped out into the crisp morning and watched the limousine head back toward

Cleary's main road. I wondered how many students would be late to school hoping for a chance to catch a glimpse of Cleary's supposed celebrity.

"This is where you grew up?" Vicken said in a dubious tone as he glanced at the houses we passed.

The quiet neighborhoods were a far stretch from New York City's busy streets. The occasional dog barked within a fenced-in backyard, and once a child of about ten took off running from his house in the direction of the elementary school; he didn't give us a second glance as he booked it down the street. I heard toll of the familiar bell and wondered if he would get detention for being late. He seemed a bit young for it, but I had spent my fair share of time in the principal's office because Drake and I often got distracted on our way to school and had to run to try to make it on time. Dad used to joke that was how I became a medal-winner in track.

"It looks nice to me," Dara said.

I caught the hint of wistfulness in her tone. Her family hadn't exactly been normal. When they found out she was an empath, they had used her to feel good about their abusive ways to the point that she refused to invite them on parent nights at school. I saw her gaze linger on the scene in a window of a mother setting her child in a high chair to eat breakfast. The smile on the mother's face as she spoke to her baby told me the loving tone I would hear if I strained to pick up her voice.

"It was a great place to grow up," I admitted. "I had a good childhood."

"It must have been hard losing your mother," Dara said with a sympathetic expression.

I nodded. "It was really hard. But Dad was always there for us, and when he married Julianne, it was good for all of us. She didn't try to take over my mom's place, she just…." I paused and realized how my throat had tightened at the words. No matter how I tried to act casual about it, talking about my mom was still hard.

"She just took a different place in the family," Dara filled in helpfully.

I threw her a grateful look. "Yes, exactly."

She slipped her hand in mine. I felt her pull gently at my sorrow. But when I shook my head, she stopped and merely walked beside me.

"I'm okay with the pain because it helps me remember how much I loved her," I said.

Dara nodded. "I'm glad you have that."

Vicken cleared his throat. "Enough of the mushy stuff. Are we almost there?"

I realized with a start that we were only a block away. "Yes. Grayson's house is just around that corner." My heart sped up at the thought of what I was about to do. I let go of Dara's hand so she wouldn't feel my anxiety.

"What's the plan?" she asked. Her eyes searched my face as if she guessed my intentions.

"Yeah, you should probably let us in on that," Vicken said wryly. "You know, so we can actually help."

I took a few more steps in silence before I said, "You're not going to like it."

"Of course we won't," the vampire replied. "When have I ever liked one of your plans?"

I let out a breath and said, "Grayson wants Vicken so he can be accepted in the Maes. The Maes has Julianne and my dad, as well as Vicken's mother, right?"

"Right," Dara said, her tone level. "So what's your plan?"

"I'm going to pretend to be Grayson."

Chapter Two

DARA AND VICKEN STOPPED walking. I turned to face them. Both of their mouths opened to protest, but I lifted a hand. "Hear me out. Grayson's whole goal is to be accepted into the Maes. The best way for me to get in is to pretend to be him and take Vicken myself. If I can get the Maes to accept me as Grayson, I'll be able to find Dad, Julianne, and Vicken's mom. It's the only way to get everyone back out."

Vicken opened his mouth again, then shut it. He looked at Dara and lifted a shoulder. "It's not a bad plan."

Dara stared from me to him. "Not a bad plan! Finn wants to willingly join the Maes and use you as leverage. Friends don't use friends as leverage. And what happens when someone finds out he's a werewolf?"

"He doesn't look like a werewolf," Vicken pointed out.

Dara sputtered and said, "What does a werewolf look like?"

Vicken shrugged. "I don't know. Not like that." He pointed at me. "He's still a bit scrawny and the girls fall over him like he's some pretty boy. I don't get it, but I definitely wouldn't think he's a werewolf to look at him." He gave me an apologetic look. "No offense."

I would take any argument in my favor at that moment. "None taken," I replied. "I agree. Nobody's going to find out I'm a werewolf if it's not a full moon. I'm getting better at my control and I'm hoping we aren't going to be there long."

"You don't even know where 'there' is," she shot back.

"That's why I need to pretend to be Grayson. It's the only way to find out where they're keeping their prisoners, or hostages, or whatever they call them." Thinking of Dad and Julianne being treated like captives made me want to phase into wolf form and tear apart anyone responsible, starting with Grayson. I shoved the impulse away before I gave Dara proof that my self-control wasn't as strong as I was implying.

"And you'd sacrifice your best friend?" Dara asked.

"Yes," Vicken said without hesitation before I could reply. "That's what best friends are for. I'd sacrifice Finn to get my mother out."

"Thanks," I said.

"No problem," he replied. "And it's worth it if we can find Finn's parents or my mother. Honestly, it's the most logical plan Finn's ever come up with."

"Thanks again," I said.

"No problem," he replied.

Dara rolled her eyes. "And where do I fit in with all of this?"

We had reached my front yard. At that moment, the door flung open and Drake ran out. The worry on my younger brother's face echoed what I was trying to keep inside. He grabbed me in a tight hug.

"Finn, you've got to find them!" he said. "You've just got to!"

I looked over his head at Dara. "You're staying with Drake."

Drake stepped back and looked at my two companions. "Uh, no way. I'm coming with you. Dad and Julianne need me."

Vicken gave a derisive snort.

Drake glared. "What do you know about it? You're the reason they're in trouble in the first place!"

"What?" Vicken asked, caught by surprise.

I shook my head. "That's not true."

"Of course it is," Drake shot back. "If Grayson didn't need a monster to get into this Mess, he wouldn't have kidnapped Julianne and Dad."

Vicken's mouth fell open, but for once he didn't have a reply.

I grabbed Drake by the shoulder and steered him toward the house.

As soon as we were inside and Dara shut the door, I said, "First of all, I'm really the monster Grayson wants to use, but for some strange sense of loyalty because of my friendship with Sebastian before he died, he chose Vicken instead. And second, they're called the Maes, not the Mess. It's an acronym for Monster Abolition and Eradication Society."

Whatever Drake was about to say fell from his lips at my words. He stared at me and said, "Monster hunters?"

I nodded.

"Monster killers," Vicken replied.

Drake stared from me to him. "So why are you here if they want to kill you?"

Vicken gave a nonchalant shrug that was belied by the shadow of worry in his yellow gaze. "Glutton for punishment, I guess."

"And you?" Drake asked, turning to Dara. "What kind of monster are you?"

"That's a little forward," I began, but Dara cut me off.

"It's alright. I'm an empath." At Drake's blank look, she explained, "I can calm people's feelings and take away their pain."

"Cool," Drake replied. "I tripped on the stairs earlier and—"

I shook my head before he could ask her to take away the pain from his bruise that he no doubt deserved. "Let's keep on topic. Drake, where's Grayson?"

"At his house, the last I heard. His parents are out of town on another business trip. He snuck over here the other night and took Dad and Julianne at gunpoint. He said he would shoot them if I called the police or did anything other than get you back here with your vampire friend." The slight waver in his voice told of how hard he was trying to keep calm.

Dara set a hand on his arm. She closed her eyes and I saw the immediate relief on Drake's face when she pulled his fear from him.

When she opened her eyes again, he was staring at her. "That. Was. Amazing. Thank you." He looked at me. "She can stay."

I fought back a smile. "I figured."

"I'm not staying," Dara replied.

"Who am I supposed to tell them you are?" I replied. "Grayson's girlfriend excited to meet monster killers?"

"Sure," she said.

"Wait. Don't tell me Finn's your boyfriend," Drake said with a note of dismay in his voice.

I cleared my throat before Dara could respond and said, "We need to focus. Let's go get Grayson, find out what he knows, and then I can find Dad and Julianne." I glanced at Vicken. "And Donessa Ruvine. We don't have time to waste." I touched Dara's arm. "Please stay. I don't know what I'd do if I brought you into danger and couldn't protect you. From what I've heard about the Maes, this isn't going to be pleasant."

"They know where we live," Drake said with a true note of concern in his voice. "I keep worrying they'll come here and take me, too."

"I'll stay," Dara finally consented.

I let out a breath of relief. "Thank you." I shot Drake a warning look. "Listen to what she says and do it exactly. Dara may be an empath, but she doesn't have sympathy for people who act stupid."

A smile appeared on Dara's face. "That's true," she confirmed.

When I closed the front door behind me, a feeling of trepidation rose in my chest. "Do you think they'll be alright?"

Vicken gave the house a glance. "They'll be safer after we deal with the Maes."

"Point taken." I took a steeling breath and nodded. "Let's find Grayson."

It turned out to be the fun part. When we reached the house, Grayson was nowhere to be found. I climbed up to the treehouse in the backyard where Drake and I had both spent countless sleepovers with Sebastian. I allowed only a slight pang of remorse for the death of my friend. Sorrow wasn't going to save my parents.

I knew before I climbed up the ladder that Grayson wasn't there, but I hoped that by looking at his notes, we might be able to figure out where to find him or, with luck, how to locate the Maes ourselves.

It took only seconds to realize that the mess of printed pictures, maps, articles on Big Foot sightings, and impressions of dog paw prints to accept that my answers wouldn't be there.

"What is this mess?" Vicken asked as he levered himself up. The look in his eyes darkened when he took in the extent of Grayson's obsession. His gaze lingered on the photograph of a wolf surfacing from the depths of a black, icy river. "Is that you?"

I nodded. "I still wonder who was sick enough to stand there and take pictures while Sebastian and Drake were drowning."

"Not to mention yourself?" Vicken pointed out levelly.

I pulled the picture down without a care for the way the pin tore it. I noticed a small thread that ran from the pin to another picture. This one showed a fuzzy photo of either a huge gray dog or a wolf standing at the edge of a children's playground. Another thread connected it to a printed picture of a black wolf standing on top of a parked car in the middle of a parking lot. I followed the thread, fascinated, as it linked pictures of what could be dogs in innocent places to obvious wolves lurking in alley shadows and even on the grounds of various schools. Several pictures came from a school written underneath as Vicki Carso's Preparatory Academy.

After that, the thread stopped. The final pin was centered on a map of New York. A big red circle marked a city block and an X was drawn on a house. The words underneath said 'Last known werewolf pack?' in big red letters.

"Is this the place Lark was talking about?" I asked.

"You know he's crazy, right?" Vicken replied.

"But what if he's not?" I asked. "What if there are more werewolves, we just don't know where to find them?"

I took down the map section and folded it up. I shoved it into my pocket. Grayson wasn't right in the head, that was certain, but if he had stumbled upon the last known location of the werewolf pack Lark had mentioned, maybe I wasn't so alone. I had so many questions about being a werewolf and no one to ask. Anything even remotely related to my heritage made professors at the Academy uncomfortable. How would it be to ask real werewolves?

"I think we should destroy this place."

I stared at Vicken. "What are you talking about?"

He waved a hand. "Look around you. If the police or anyone else finds it, they're going to start asking their own questions. This Grayson may be crazy, but he's gathered enough information here to clue others in on the monsters that are out there."

Glancing around, I had to admit that he was right. "What are you suggesting?"

Vicken pulled a lighter from his pocket. "Burn it."

I stared at him. "Where did you get a lighter, and aren't vampires afraid of fire?"

Vicken tossed it to me. "I stole it from your brother, and I'm not going to light it, you are."

The tiny lighter felt innocuous in my hand. "I'm lighting it?"

Vicken headed back to the ladder with a speed that told of true fear. "Yes, but wait until after I get down."

Another thought struck me. "Why did my brother have a lighter?"

"Maybe he's a pyro?" Vicken suggested as his head disappeared down the hatch.

The suggestion that my brother was a pyromaniac didn't rest well with me. I shook my head and stared around the treehouse, wondering where the best place would be to start the fire. I debated whether my werewolf side was to blame for my reluctance to do so. I had never been obsessed with fire like so many kids my age were growing up. When two of my friends were taken in for questioning for starting the old fairgrounds on fire by accident, I had been busy building model cars and watching Drake play baseball. Even Dad had laughed at the suggestion that I had been involved.

Wolves definitely didn't like fire. I figured my aversion to demon fire had been purely survival, but now, as I flicked the lighter and touched the flame to one of Grayson's hundreds of papers, I realized it came from something deeply inborn. Perhaps vampires and werewolves weren't that different from each other.

"Are you trying to burn yourself alive?" Vicken shouted from below.

"I'm waiting to see if you'll come rescue me if I'm up here long enough," I replied.

Vicken muttered a series of curses strung together in a way that would have made even Professor Briggs blush.

I ensured the fire was well started before hightailing it down the ladder.

"About time," Vicken grumbled. "Let's get out of here before the firemen show up."

"What about Grayson?" I asked.

"I have a feeling he's going to be very concerned about who started the fire. Our goal is to find him before the police do. Time to put your nose to work."

I couldn't help the astonishment that filled my face at his suggestion. "Phase to wolf form in broad daylight? What if somebody sees me?"

"They'll think wolves have returned to Cleary," Vicken replied. "Or be fast enough that they don't see you. We need

Grayson, and you're the fastest way to finding him. Get to work, hound."

His demanding tone made me want to bare my teeth. I had never phased during the day before. I grabbed onto the urge to snarl at the vampire and went with it. A glance at the treehouse showed smoke just beginning to filter between the branches. We had minutes at the most. I pulled off my shirt, but couldn't get the phase to begin.

"Say something else to make me mad," I told Vicken.

He lifted a shoulder. "That's easy. You have fleas."

I rolled my eyes. "No. Something real. I need to want to fight."

Understanding dawned in his eyes. He crossed his arms and planted his feet as though bracing for an attack.

"Werewolves are the bane of monster existence. They should have been wiped from the world long ago."

A tremor of what felt like electricity ran down my spine. I wanted to knock the superior look from his face and teach him that to disrespect my ancestors was akin to looking death in the eyes.

He continued with, "Your kind is a scourge, a virus. You are merely animals trapped in the bodies of humans, waiting to tear apart anyone who gets in your way."

The suggestion was the trigger for my phase. I dropped to all fours and allowed the change to take over. Fur, muscles, fangs, and eyesight all shifted within seconds. When I looked up in my wolf form, I took satisfaction in the way Vicken backed off a step before he could stop himself.

"You want me to keep going?" he asked with forced bravado in his tone. "I have more I could say."

I snarled an answer. Even though I knew he had said those things because I asked him, I couldn't help feeling as though he had come up with what he said far too easily. If he was harboring such feelings about my kind, wouldn't they pertain to me as well? Could I really trust a vampire to guard my back if he felt werewolves were a scourge?

I had to remind myself that he was taking even more of a risk than I was in meeting the Maes. I might be in disguise, but he was heading into the fray with everyone knowing his vampire heritage. He was the one who needed to trust me. If he could do that after all he had said about werewolves, who was I to argue?

I circled the treehouse and found Grayson's scent. In wolf form, I could smell the hint of insanity in the tangle of smells that made up his individual odor. It made my lips pull back in a snarl of distaste. During my last interaction with him, I'd had suspicions about whether he was crazy; now I knew for sure. The thought of Dad and Julianne under his control made me so upset I could barely keep to a pace Vicken could match.

"More running," I heard him say behind me. "Seriously. Can't you trail the guy without running? We look more than a little suspicious. What's more suspicious than a wolf being chased by a vampire? Nothing, that's what. Nothing. Slow down, weremutt!"

The stick he threw hit my paws with painful accuracy and sent me sprawling into a fence. I rose fueled with adrenaline and the rage I still harbored at his words. At that moment, with my heart pounding in my ears and the thrill of the chase still pushing me, I felt more wolf than human. I snapped at the enemy who had brought me down instead of allowing me to continue my hunt.

Vicken knocked my muzzle aside with a slap that was hard enough to make my head ring; in the same smooth motion, he slipped behind me and locked a hand under my jaw. He put his other arm behind my head and pulled my head up and back to the point that stars danced in front of my eyes.

"Want to try biting me again, Finn?" he hissed in my ear.

The intensity of his tone sent a shiver running down my spine. I knew that he could easily snap my neck and I wouldn't be able to do anything about it. One move, and everything I tried to accomplish would vanish. Vicken had all the power, and I had given it to him through sheer stupidity.

Though my wolf instincts screamed for me to do otherwise, I chose the only course of action I had. I pulled my ears back against my skull, closed my eyes, let my tail slink between my legs, and I whined. It was perhaps the most humiliating moment of my entire life.

Vicken let me go the moment the sound left my throat. He backed away quickly with his hands out as though he didn't know what to do with them. I rose shakily to my feet and watched him, my muscles tense and stance wary.

Vicken sucked in a breath and then let it out as though he didn't know what to say. He finally broke the silence with, "I, uh, guess we can both chalk that down to nerves, wouldn't you say?"

I nodded since it was the only way I could respond in my wolf form.

"Alright then," the vampire replied. He gestured in the direction I had been running, but did so with his chin instead of his hands as though he was ashamed of them. His voice was quiet when he said, "We'd better get going, I guess."

It took every bit of courage I had to let him walk beside me. I knew distance was my best friend. The speed Vicken had shown was terrifying, and his strength made my wolf form feel paltry at best. It wasn't a sensation I was used to. Since finding out I was a werewolf, the strength that came with it appeared in spurts and strange surges, but it made me feel strong, at least in my human form. I was starting to realize that while there were advantages to being a wolf, the strength wasn't there when I needed it. I made a mental note to ask Professor Briggs about it when, or if, we made it back to Haunted High.

"You know I wouldn't really hurt you," Vicken said after we had walked several blocks.

I glanced up at him. He had his hands in the pockets of his long black coat, something I had never seen him do before. I wondered how close he had really come to pulling my neck back far enough to hear it crack. The thought wasn't a pleasant one.

I could hear the sirens of fire engines as they headed to the Newton house. They wouldn't get there in time to save the treehouse, but hopefully they could keep it from spreading anywhere else. The thought of our childhood playhouse up in flames made my heart ache. It was one more thing of Sebastian's that slipped through the cracks, and it was my fault. If he hadn't died in the car accident, Grayson would have no reason to want to join the Maes or even know about them. I vowed to make that part right at least.

His scent became fresh when we neared the gas station at the far edge of Cleary. I paused near the line of scrawny trees that separated it from the tire repair shop. Vicken leaned around a tree to see where I was looking.

"Is that him?" he whispered.

I nodded. The sight of Grayson working behind the counter at the gas station as though it was just another day made my hackles rise. Nobody else was there at the moment and Grayson appeared to be busy with whatever task he performed. His red hair stood up in the same unruly way Sebastian's had, but his football player build was the opposite of how slender Bast had been. I missed my friend and the appearance of his brother filled me with regret and anger for how he had retaliated against my family for something that had been an accident.

I didn't know I was growling until Vicken set a hand on my back.

"Easy. We have to be smart about this," he warned quietly.

I nudged my nose toward his backpack where my clothes were.

Vicken shook his head. "I have a better idea. Wait around back."

He left the cover of the trees and headed straight for the gas station. I wanted to call him back, but couldn't. The look of vengeance on his face should have worried me, but I wanted a piece of Grayson myself. I slipped around the back and stood anxiously by the door. I heard the bell on the front door ring when Vicken entered. Leaning close to the crack, I listened to Grayson's bored welcome followed by a few pointed words from the vampire. Grayson shouted something, items crashed to the floor, and then the sound of footsteps running toward the back made me take a few steps to the side.

Grayson flew through the door as though the devil was on his heels. I caught a glimpse of Vicken, his fangs elongated for feeding and a look of pure rage on his face, and realized that maybe the devil truly was. The smell of Grayson's fear combined with his instability brought my growl from a rumble to a roar. Grayson stopped three feet from the door. He looked from me to Vicken and back again.

"H-hi Finn," he said, his voice shaking. "I see Drake got you my m-message."

I closed the space between us and bared my fangs completely.

Grayson's hands flew up. "Okay, okay, I'll admit I didn't think this through. I'm sorry I took your parents."

"Where are they?" Vicken demanded.

Grayson glanced back at the vampire, his eyes bright with terror. "Th-the Maes has them for testing."

A shard of fear shot through me. I snapped at him, closing my teeth within inches of his thigh. He jumped and tears filled his eyes.

"I'm so sorry!" he said.

"Why are they testing them?" Vicken demanded, giving voice to my questions.

"B-because of him," Grayson replied, pointing to me. His finger shook.

Vicken crossed his arms. "That makes no sense. His mother was the werewolf, not his father. His dad and Julianne are both human."

Grayson shook his head so quickly I was amazed it didn't give him whiplash. "They said if Finn is an Alpha, both bloodlines have to carry the gene."

Vicken and I stared at each other. If what Grayson said was true, Dad, Julianne, and Juli's unborn baby could be in serious trouble.

Vicken grabbed Grayson's arm and hauled him back inside the gas station. He set the backpack on the floor and shoved Grayson ahead of him.

"Close up shop. We need to have a conversation," the vampire said in a level, ominous tone.

Chapter Three

"YOU'RE LUCKY ALL THEIR communication with Grayson was digital," Vicken pointed out as we waited near the Cleary city sign.

"I think I could pass off as a six foot three red-headed jock drop out, don't you?" I asked.

"Maybe if we kill a fox and make you wear it for a hat, and then tell them you've been starving yourself on some new fad vegetable diet I hear humans are crazy about. It's not right. Carnivores needs to eat meat, fresh meat."

I stared at him. "What is it with you about wanting to kill things?"

He lifted a shoulder in a nonchalant shrug. "I'm a vampire. It's the circle of life and all that."

I shook my head. "It's sick. That's what it is."

"You wanted to kill Grayson."

"That's different. He kidnapped my parents. Don't you want to hurt the person who took your mom?"

Vicken fell silent. We both brooded as we anxiously awaited the arrival of the Maes.

I didn't know what to expect. Grayson said under their orders he had left Dad and Julianne knocked out by chloroform and tied up behind the sign. They had strictly prohibited him to stay, saying only that they would contact him if his offering was enough. When they emailed back stating that they needed a pureblood monster, he had promised Drake our parents back if he would tell him about my monster friends. I couldn't hold it against Drake for giving in; he was as desperate to see our parents safe as I was.

This time, the Maes had responded far faster, according to Grayson. As soon as he sent a picture of Vicken tied up and unconscious the way we had staged him to be, with his mouth slightly open to show his fangs, they had written back immediately and asked to meet. I waited in Grayson's letterman jacket from Cleary High. The voice in the back of my mind noted that I would have received one of my own at the end of the year in track if I had stayed. I pushed the thought aside and watched the road.

A small white car appeared in the distance. I waited in silence as it neared the sign and slowed.

"I've been around vampires for too long," I muttered under my breath. "I was expecting a limousine."

"What is it?" Vicken asked from his place on the ground.

Glancing down, I would have guessed he was unconscious. I had to give the vampire credit for looking even more dead than usual. His head lolled to the side and his chest barely rose with each breath.

"A white car. Small. Older looking." I glanced down at him. "Like you right now."

"Bite me, weremutt."

"Poor word choice coming from a vampire," I muttered.

He grabbed my ankle faster than I could respond. I fell against the sign with an oomph.

"Are you alright?" a wary voice asked.

I looked up to see that a man and a woman had left the car. A quick glance at Vicken showed him to be as lifeless as ever. I resisted the urge to kick him.

"I, uh, tripped." Fortunately, from the correspondence Grayson had shown us, his spelling was poor, his grammar even worse, and his efforts to be stealthy had been bumbling at best. I could act like an idiot and get away with it. I gave a stupid grin and held out a hand. "I'm Grayson Newton. It's about time you guys got here."

The woman's tone showed her annoyance when she said, "I'm Eileen and this is Mangus. We came as quickly as we could. You need to understand that there are protocols we have to follow with this sort of thing."

Mangus' attention was entirely on Vicken. He walked carefully toward the vampire. My heart slowed at the sight of a gun in his hand.

"You didn't say anything about shooting him," I said. I was careful to keep my tone level despite the way my heart thundered in my chest.

To Vicken's credit, he didn't twitch at all at the mention of the weapon.

"Precautionary measures," Mangus said over his shoulder without taking his eyes from Vicken. "You don't want to know what happens when a vampire wakes up in a strange car. It's a mess for everyone, and Madam Opal doesn't appreciate messes."

I knew better than to ask who Madam Opal was, but I filed the name away for later.

"Unfortunately, Madam Opal only allows us to use stunners on the beasts. It'd be more fun if we could wing them or something," Mangus said.

He took aim at Vicken and fired. A small ball pegged the vampire in the chest, opened like the legs of a spider, then sunk the legs into his skin. Vicken's eyes flew open as a surge of white electricity flowed over his body. His back arched and a gasp escaped his lips before the electricity faded. He crumpled to the ground in a motionless heap.

I had to stop myself from running to his side. Only the reminder that my parents' lives depended on acting like Grayson kept me frozen to the spot.

"I still like seeing them squirm," Eileen said with a half-smile as the man hoisted Vicken's body onto his shoulder.

She pressed the trunk release on the key she held and the trunk of the car popped open. Mangus unceremoniously dropped Vicken inside and slammed the trunk shut.

"Well, you coming, Grayson?"

I realized the woman had opened one of the doors to the backseat of the car and was standing beside it with an impatient expression. I hurried over and ducked inside before I could second-guess my actions. Eileen shut the door and walked around to the driver's seat. Mangus slid onto the passenger seat. He grabbed something from the floor and held it back to me.

I looked at the black cloth but didn't take it.

"Come on," Mangus said as Eileen pulled onto the road. "Put it over your head. If you take it off, I've got permission to shoot you, too."

I took the cloth, opened it to find that it was a sack of sorts, and put it over my head. The scent of someone else's breath made my nose wrinkle, but I didn't take it off. I sat in my seat and listened to the hum of the tires over the road. Someone turned the radio to an oldies station. I tried to listen to the words to keep my mind from my best friend who had been electrocuted and thrown into the trunk. This trip was already going differently than I had planned.

I had no idea how much time had passed before the car slowed. The car turned and the sound of the asphalt changed. The brakes squeaked when we came to a complete stop. My heart raced as my door was opened.

"You can remove the sack now," Eileen said.

I pulled it off and looked from her to the building behind her. Night had fallen during our trip and the structure I looked at was lit by hundreds of lights around the outside. The inside glowed brightly as well. The familiarity of the building struck me.

"Is that a mall?" I asked.

Eileen glanced behind her. "It *was* a mall. Now it's the Society's headquarters."

I refrained from questioning why an organization like the Maes would want to have their headquarters in an abandoned mall.

Mangus opened the trunk and slung Vicken's still body over his shoulder. I followed behind them watching intently for any sign of life from the vampire. My ears caught the sound of his slow heartbeat as we neared the doors and I let out a sigh of relief. I wondered anxiously how long he would be out. Neither of us had counted on him being unconscious when we entered the compound.

My muscles tensed at the sight of men and women standing guard at the entrance. I remembered that I was supposed to be Grayson. If I didn't get keep in character, Vicken's odds of getting out alive would be zero.

"So, uh, a mall; that's cool I guess."

Eileen shot me a glance. "When you see why, you'll understand. For now, keep your trap shut."

I figured Grayson would probably take that advice, especially with guns pointed casually at him. Though their fingers weren't on the triggers, the guards' ready stances left no doubt they would shoot me given any reason. When they pulled the doors open at Eileen's nod, I could feel their eyes on my back.

Scents assailed my nose as I followed Mangus and Eileen up the wide corridor. I quickly saw why Eileen had said the mall would make sense as the Maes' headquarters. The separate stores that normally took up each side of the long entrance hallway had been changed into cages. Bars ran from the ceiling to the floor where the windows used to be. The only visible furniture was a mattress on the floor and a corner sectioned off with a sheet that I assumed was for bathroom needs. With the overhead lights glaring down, there was nowhere for the occupants to hide.

A woman with long white hair and white eyes peered at me from her seat on the middle of her bed. A shiver ran down my spine at the sight of sorrow and dejection in her eyes. In the next cage, a man dressed only in shorts was covered from head to toe in orange scales. He looked like he could be related to Fren from my Care of Green Multicellular Organisms class. The thought made my stomach tighten.

A glance ahead of us showed two levels and branching hallways filled with similar cages. I wondered uneasily if they were all occupied. Eileen led us to an escalator and we rode up it.

"Why are there so many cages?" I asked.

Mangus grunted from where he carried Vicken over his shoulder. "Madam Opal is a collector."

At my stare, Eileen grinned. "Interesting, right? She likes to display the various species we could run into out there so members of the Society will be ready to act if they see one. If your contribution," she nodded at where Vicken hung motionless down Mangus' back, "Is pure blood, he may be added to her display; otherwise, he'll be one of the lucky ones."

I kept my tone level when I asked, "What do you mean by lucky?"

Eileen shrugged. "If he's not chosen for display, he'll be put in the training range for new Maes to test out their skills. With any luck, he won't suffer much before he dies."

I forced myself to ask, "Why is staying on display not lucky?"

Eileen and Mangus exchanged grins. "Because those on display are also the test subjects for the various stun weapons Madam Opal lets the children use." She pointed at a cage we passed. The young man inside sat with his back to the corridor. He was bare from the waist up and red marks marred his skin. "A lot of the weapons are still being tested. I've heard that they sting a bit."

At her words, the young man turned his head to look at us. His head twisted on his neck owl-like so that he didn't have to turn his shoulders at all. His eyes were yellow-orange and bright like fire, and the look in them was filled with such hatred and rage I was amazed the bars didn't melt.

Eileen didn't appear to notice the man's anger. She walked passed without a second glance, but when I looked back, I saw the man's head turn back slowly and his shoulders hunch in defeat. The image stayed in my mind as I followed the others down up hall.

The silence set my teeth on edge. Instead of a howling, angry, demanding horde of captives, they sat silently as though they had either given up or there was a punishment for making noise. Interspersed along the hallways and cages were guards with guns who stood still as if used to doing so for long shifts. I wondered how often they rotated through the day.

I wasn't surprised to see the occasional demon standing near the guards. Their kind would be drawn to such a place where pain was used to create order. I ignored their glowering stares and followed the others to the wide room at the far end. The guards barely glanced at me when they opened the iron-barred door for us to pass. I wondered if they got a good deal on bars when they remodeled the place.

The faint scent of new clothes and shoes still lingered, but only the carpet of the department store remained. In the place of clothing and purse displays, rows of bleachers had been built, and at the far end, a long table surrounded by leather chairs made up the only other furniture. For all the space they had, they definitely didn't put much effort into decorating.

Eight individuals occupied the table, four on the side facing us, three with their backs to us, and at the head of the table sat a woman with white hair tucked into a tight bun. Demons sat at their feet and on the table, but the humans ignored them. They appeared to be in deep discussion. Eileen and Mangus waited a respectful distance away for them to finish talking. It wasn't hard to overhear their conversation even though we were far enough away that I doubted the other two could hear.

"In order to keep the warlock population manageable, I'm proposing a sweep of the entire eastern side. Our targets are getting sparse in the city section. I'm sure Sir Harbrand would welcome the additions."

The woman at the head of the table said, "All those in favor of granting Sir Anderson militia in order to complete his proposal, say yes."

A series of yeses followed.

"All those against?"

Nobody spoke.

The woman nodded. "Sir Anderson, your proposal is granted. Check with Sir Harbrand about the number of refills he needs."

"Thank you, Madam Opal. I appreciate your consideration. Sir Harbrand will have the additions as soon as I return."

The woman nodded. "The Society has your gratitude, Sir Anderson."

He put his hand to his heart and gave a strange little bow before he took his seat at the table once more.

"What is this, some kind of king's court session?" I asked with a sarcasm that matched Grayson's. "This is really weird."

Eileen elbowed me in the ribs. "Quiet, or they'll send you out for target practice."

"Let the boy speak," Madam Opal said, raising her voice.

Every eye turned to me.

Reminding myself that I was supposed to be Grayson, I cleared my throat and said, "No disrespect, ma'am, but I was hoping to be a part of this society; I just didn't know what I was getting into."

Disapproval filled the room. No one at the table needed to speak to let me know that I had just offended every one of them on some deep level. I caught myself fidgeting with the hem of my shirt and willed my hands to still; perhaps I had pushed it too far.

The woman rose from her seat at the head of the table. She wore a high-collared starched white shirt and flowing dress pants with heeled boots that clicked when she walked. Taking stately steps, she stalked with her head held high and several demons shadowing her path. She ignored Mangus who still stood there with Vicken on his shoulder, the cords of his neck standing out with the obvious strain, and stopped in front of me. I had a clear view of the gun she wore on a black holster at her belt. The strap of the holster had been cut off to give quicker access to the weapon. By the way the grip was worn smooth, I knew it was used often.

An uncomfortable silence filled the room as she waited for something. I didn't know what to say and had already pressed my luck too far, so I chose not to speak.

Someone from the table cleared his throat pointedly.

"Oh, um, yes," Eileen said with clear embarrassment on her face. "Madam Opal, this is Grayson Newton, the boy who wants to join our Society."

"Lackeys," a man from the table muttered. Quiet laughter followed the remark, only to cut off at Madam Opal's glance.

Madam Opal looked me up and down. I ignored the urge to shift my weight from foot to foot. She finally turned her attention to Mangus.

"I suppose this is your offering?" she said.

It took me a moment to realize she was speaking to me.

"Uh, yes, yes, this is the vampire I told you about," I replied. At another cleared throat, I concluded with, "Madam."

She walked around Mangus, looking at Vicken without touching him. I hoped for the vampire's sake that he was still stunned. I didn't want either of us to look down the barrel of her pistol.

At one point, she grabbed Vicken's long black hair that had come free of his usual ponytail and used it to lift his head so that she could check out his teeth. She then let his head go and it fell against Mangus' back.

"A nice specimen," she concluded with a satisfactory nod. She turned to face me again. "Much better than the others you sent to us. It'll be years before we know if that one pays off."

Before I had a chance to ask what she meant, she continued with, "Though I would still reward you handsomely if you could get your hands on that werewolf. A prize like that would make a fantastic display; unfortunately, the Academy is too heavily warded for us to get inside." She gave a sigh as if this was a true shame, then gestured to Vicken and said, "But if you're correct and this is indeed the son of Don Ruvine, you will be pleasantly rewarded. We've been waiting positively ages for a specimen of this quality." She motioned to Mangus. "Have him tested. If he's Don Ruvine the Third, put him on the main display."

"And if not?" Mangus asked, his voice tight and shoulders bowed under the strain of carrying the vampire.

Madam Opal gave another wave of her hand as she walked away from him. "Hand him over to Sir Harbrand. I've heard our last vampire's head was obliterated in yesterday's session. Pity. She held up well."

I caught the slightest twitch of Vicken's fingers at Madam Opal's words. I wondered if she had just spoken her own death sentence with her flippancy at the life of a vampire. When Mangus walked out of the room without retaliation, I knew only the thought of Vicken's mother kept him from reacting. The voice in the back of my mind asked if they were talking about his mother. A wave of nausea swept over me at the thought.

"Approach the table, Grayson Newton."

I started with a jerk at the realization that she meant me. It took considerable effort to turn away from the closing doors and cross to the table. Eileen stood with her hands behind her back and her eyes on the ground as though it was against the rules to look at Madam Opal without being spoken to first. It was all I could do to keep the defiance from my face when I reached the table.

I knew I should wait to be address. Because of that, I spoke first. "This is a pretty cool place you've got here."

I watched everyone stare from me to Madam Opal. The clear outrage at my lack of manners seemed far more shocking than it should have been.

Madam Opal was the only one who didn't appear to take immediate offense. She sat with a grace that nearly matched the smoothness of a vampire and looked up only after her dress pants had been arranged to her liking.

"Young man, you are in the presence of the High Members of the Monster Abolition and Eradication Society. When you are here, you will address each Member as Sir or Madam, you will not make vocal observations like, 'This is a pretty cool place you've got here.' You will also not speak unless spoken to." Madam Opal's flinty gaze gave no spark of humor when she concluded with, "And if you fail to uphold these standards, your tongue and your eyes will be removed and you will be taken to the training grounds as a target of no more value than your vampire, should he prove to be of less than noble blood."

The astonishment on my face wasn't faked. At the silence that followed her words, I didn't know whether to speak or wait. At the risk of losing it, I held my tongue.

Madam Opal gave a nod of approval. "Very well, Grayson. I'm glad to see that you are a quick learner. You may be of some use to our Society yet."

I opened my mouth, then shut it again.

Madam Opal motioned with one finger. "You may speak."

"Th-thank you," I said in what I hoped was an imitation of how Grayson would reaction under such circumstances. "I am, um, honored, to be here and, um, grateful, for the chance to meet you fine people."

The corner of Madam Opal's mouth turned up in a small smile. "Thank you, Grayson. We're hoping that you will fit in here. Keep in mind that it won't be easy, but if you stay loyal to the Society and work hard, you will be rewarded."

The same man cleared his throat. I wanted to throttle him.

Madam Opal bowed her head in acknowledgement. "Grayson, we have things to attend to here. I'm sure Eileen would be happy to show you around. When you are settled in, you'll report to Sir Harbrand for training."

I gave an awkward bow and stuttered, "Th-thank you, Madam Opal. I won't let you down."

It took every ounce of strength I possessed to walk away from that table instead of phasing and letting the wolf side of me teach a lesson to those snide murderers as I so wished to do. With every step, I promised vengeance for those who had fallen at their merciless hands. But first, I had to find Dad and Julianne and ensure that they were safe. I couldn't do anything else until they were out of harm.

Chapter Four

"IT'S PRETTY SIMPLE HERE," Eileen told me as I followed her. "Keep to yourself, don't bother the displays, don't speak to the High Members unless spoken to, and do what you're told."

"Sounds simple enough," I replied. I remembered at the last minute to add one of Grayson's sarcastic, "And if I forget? Do I lose an eye or something?"

The gaze Eileen turned on me was flat when she said, "A knuckle each time." She held up her left hand. I noticed for the first time that her pinky and her ring finger were both missing from the first knuckle up.

I wasn't acting when my mouth fell open. "That's a little harsh, don't you think?"

She didn't let how she felt about it show when she replied, "You learn quickly."

With my stomach twisted in knots, I followed her back down the corridor. She led us to another expansive hallway where an escalator led to the first floor. I stepped on it without a word and she did the same. When we reached the ground, she walked past the displays on either side as though she didn't see them. I looked in each cage hoping to find Dad and Julianne, but the dejected gazes of the mythics inside met me instead.

Flashbacks of the Mythic Labs beneath the park in New York flooded my mind. I was the one behind the cage watching Stith torture Professor Briggs. I saw Vicken dying as the venom of the demon bite turned his blood against him. I was on the table again. Dr. Fagrin was ordering his men to break my arm so they could document how it healed in the moonlight. Then I was fighting the Wiccan Enforcer, the demon who took over the doctor's body. Chanting filled the air. I wasn't alone.

"Are you coming?"

My head jerked up when I found myself standing in the middle of the hall, my vision torn between the past and the present.

"Cages," I said, still trying to make sense of where I was.

Eileen crossed back to me. "Grayson, what's going on?"

The name she called me tore me back to the present-day. I searched my mind quickly for something to say that would alleviate the confusion I read on her face. How would I explain post-traumatic stress hallucinations about torture and demons to a woman who clearly didn't see the demons following her own path?

"I, uh, was admiring the cages. It's a great design," I said belatedly.

Eileen nodded as though she didn't think I was as crazy as I felt. "I told you you'd understand why Madam Opal commandeered the mall. Some of us thought she was crazy, but after her vision was carried out, it made perfect sense." She winked at me. "It's not so bad here." She set a hand on my arm. "Come on, I'll show you the ropes."

Outwardly I kept my expression calm but inside my stomach writhed at the realization that she was flirting with me. Hopefully, it would be enough to cover up any slipups I made. I knew I was lucky to get away with drifting off once like that, but I couldn't count on such luck holding out.

I tried to sound nonchalant when I asked, "What did Madam Opal mean when she said it'll be years before they know if my last contribution to her display will pay off?"

Eileen gave a bored shrug. "Testing and all that. Apparently, the male was a carrier of the werewolf gene, but it's dormancy was confirmed."

I asked the question I dreaded. "How did they confirm that?"

"The usual way," Eileen replied. "He was beaten until he would have changed form to defend himself. He didn't change into a wolf, so no go." She glanced at me and misread my expression. "Don't feel bad you judged that one wrong; there's still hope. The little one might still prove to be a monster instead of just a carrier."

I stopped walking entirely. "What little one?"

Her eyebrows lifted as she studied me, and then a light came to her eyes. "Oh, you wouldn't have any way to know, would you? The baby was born. Now it's just a matter of waiting until the creature reaches puberty to see if it'll turn into a wolf like its older brother. It's too bad it won't be an Alpha. Sir Harbrand already confirmed that the woman wasn't a carrier of the werewolf gene. More's the pity."

She kept talking, but I didn't hear what she said. Her words, 'The baby was born,' kept repeating over and over in my mind. Julianne and Dad's baby, my half-brother or sister, was somewhere in this facility locked away so they could wait and see whether or not the werewolf gene would dominate. The thought made me sick.

It was only with utmost concentration that I kept my emotions from my voice when I asked, "Where are they?"

"The training grounds," Eileen replied.

I strained against the wolf that fought to tear her from limb to limb at her casual tone. "And where is that?"

My tight voice must have caught her attention because she gave me a closer look. "The parking area beneath the mall was turned into Sir Harbrand's training grounds when they remodeled the place. I usually don't show newbies the training facilities until tomorrow when you report for your first day, but I guess I could make an exception seeing how you brought the others here."

I nodded and was grateful when she took that as my answer because I no longer trusted my voice.

"From what I heard, the woman hasn't been doing very well since the baby was born," she said conversationally as I followed her along the first floor. "One of the newbies said both the man and woman didn't fight much when shot at during training last night. Sir Harbrand doesn't give them long, especially if the man keeps sacrificing himself to protect the woman. The trainees' bullets are weaker, but the heart can only handle so much electricity, you know?"

She looked back at me as if expecting a reply. I was so close to phasing I could only snarl, "I'll bet."

"Are you alright?" she asked as we reached a second set of escalators. "You don't look so good." She nodded at the armed guards standing at each end and they waved us on.

I cleared my throat and gave her a weak smile. "I'm fine. Long day."

She nodded and gave a flick of her hand to indicate the exhibits we left behind. "This place is pretty overwhelming, and it was a long trip. Maybe we should wait for tomorrow before we go to the training grounds."

"No," I said too quickly. At her surprised expression, I took a calming breath and continued with, "I'd like to see where they ended up. They were hard to catch, you know?"

She nodded as if that made perfect sense. I breathed a sigh of relief and watched the main floor disappear above our heads.

The scent of the next floor hit me hard. I blinked at the sharpness of the fear and pain that wafted up the escalator. It set my teeth on edge as reminders of the Mythic Labs pressed against me. Adrenaline raced through my veins and it was all I could do to walk sedately beside Eileen when we reached the parking garage. Fortunately, the guards waved us on when Eileen showed them her security pass. I didn't know how I would react if they tried to stop us.

"I'm sure Mangus and Sir Harbrand are busy with that new vampire. The testing process takes some time," Eileen said.

"What do they do?" I asked through clenched teeth.

This floor of the parking garage appeared normal. Gray walls, cement pillars, and even the faded stripes where the parking places had been still remained. Even so, my instincts warned that it wasn't a safe place. Guards were spaced throughout the garage and I could feel their eyes on me when we passed by. I refused to let my guard down as I followed Eileen around to the next escalator. She swiped her card on the reader and the escalator started down. The voice in the back of my mind noted ironically that without her card, the escalator was still a set of stairs we could just descend.

"Blood tests to begin with," she replied. "Sir Harbrand knows how to identify the specific genes he's looking for. I don't know. Something about DNA strands and genetic markers." She toyed with her hair. "They keep me around because I'm good with a gun, not blood."

I forced out the reply, "They're lucky to have you."

She threw me a bright smile. "Thanks, Grayson. They're lucky to have you here now, too! I think we'll make a good team."

"Me, too," I replied.

She gave a little giggle and blushed. I had no idea if she was pretty. She may have been a tree nymph crossed with a slimy-skinned taniwha entomophage, in other words, not a pretty sight, but I wouldn't have known the difference for all the attention I paid her. She didn't seem to notice because she continued to giggle and flirt and twirl her hair as we rode down the next escalator.

My attention was taken by the difference in levels. The next one was twice as deep and for a brief moment, the escalator gave us a view of the entire area. Where the last one had been normal and gray, this one had been turned into a myriad of manmade landscapes. In front of me, I could see the browns and greens of a painted forest; to the right were wooden panels painted to look like a cityscape; to the left was the inside of a shopping center, complete with aisles and shopping carts; and behind us, just before the view disappeared as we rode down, I saw a neighborhood laid out with houses and streets.

The need for Eileen's security card became apparent when we reached the glass enclosure at the bottom of the escalator. There was no way out except through the set of doors in front of us. She waved her card at the reader and the doors opened.

"Welcome to the training grounds," she announced as proudly as if she had built it with her own two hands. Her smug look vanished at my expression. "Grayson, are you sure you're alright?"

I wasn't. I felt like I was about to vomit. The scents of agony that hit me were so strong my stomach roiled. Everywhere I looked, demon shadows wandered. It was no wonder they were attracted to the area. If I was a demon, I would have been perfectly happy there. Thoughts of Chutka the Shambler and the demons we had faced to try to stop him swarmed my mind. I could see the flame-filled eyes of the demon hordes we had left in Lark's basement. One bite had been enough to nearly kill Vicken. What would happen if we couldn't stop Chutka from reaching our world with the rest of his horde?

Eileen set a hand on my shoulder, jarring me back to the present. "I'm, uh, fine. I think I just ate something bad." I remembered at the last minute that I was supposed to be Grayson and added, "Who knew a box of donuts on an empty stomach was a bad idea?"

She laughed as though I had said the funniest thing in the world. "You're cute, you know that?" she asked. She winked at me. "Let's go find those creatures you brought in."

I followed her numbly through the training grounds. Men and women in black uniforms with padded armor and automatic weapons nodded when we walked by. I soon saw the reason for their diligence.

Monsters were chained at every junction. Most slumped against the walls or slept on the floors as though exhausted from the last training bout. On each one, I could see the angry welts where they had been hit by electric bullets like the spider one Mangus had used on Vicken. The freshest bullet marks were easy to tell by the way they blistered and oozed. It looked incredibly painful and I felt bad for those monsters who didn't have the ability to heal quickly.

The monsters who were still awake turned away from us or ducked their heads when we passed.

"Don't worry. It's a bit more lively down here during the training sessions," Eileen informed me. "They're encouraged to either try to attack the trainees, which of course they can't because of their chains, or to try to hide so the trainees have to seek them out. They know better than to laze around like this if they don't want to feel Sir Harbrand's wrath, right wretch?"

She kicked the foot of a sleeping woman. The woman startled and jumped back to the length of her chain. There was so much fear in her eyes that were cat-like and reminded me of Adalia and Melzie from Mrs. Mellon's class. The woman didn't say a word, but the expectation of pain on her face ate at my self-control.

Eileen pulled a baton from her belt that sparked with electricity when she pushed a button. She took a step toward the woman. The woman opened her mouth in a soundless hiss that showed pointed canines, but she couldn't get any further away from us. The metal manacle around her neck showed raw skin where she had already fought to get free and failed. Seeing a woman turned into less than an animal by the Society's cruelty set my teeth on edge.

"Leave her alone," I said before I could stop myself.

"Why?" Eileen asked; her tone was suspicious.

I searched quickly for an answer. "If, uh, she isn't rested, she won't give a good performance for the trainees tomorrow. We want to make sure the trainees are well trained, right? And that includes me, now. I've got to get good at this stuff." Eileen watched me for a moment with a skeptical expression on her face. I gave her my best smile and continued with, "Besides, I'd rather talk to you than watch you torture her."

My smile seemed to do the trick. She shrugged. "Can't argue with that. I'm enjoying our conversation as well."

To my relief, she clicked the button on her baton again and the electricity shut off. The woman with the cat eyes watched us warily as Eileen slid the baton back onto her belt. I felt the woman's eyes on us when we turned away and walked deeper into the training labyrinth.

"This place is huge," I said. "How do trainees keep from getting lost?"

She eyed a chained man who appeared to be normal as he slept except for the way his hands and feet moved like a dog chasing a rabbit in his dreams.

"I got lost my first time down here," she admitted. "It's a huge place." She shot me an embarrassed look. "I got trapped into a corner by a vampire. His chain was just short enough that he couldn't reach me, but I couldn't get past him. I was out of bullets and didn't know how to use my baton. It was pathetic."

I tried to sound sincere when I said, "You must have been terrified. How did you get out?"

"They had to come rescue me," she admitted. "Sir Harbrand didn't let me live that down for a week. He made me wash out the body bags after they burned the bodies of the monsters killed during the training. It was disgusting."

I swallowed the bile that surged into my throat at her words. It was disgusting, but not in the way she implied. Monsters had died here at the hands of trainees being trained to kill them. I didn't know how it felt to die from surges of electricity, but I knew it couldn't be pleasant. The lingering scent of charred flesh touched my nose. It was almost enough to send me over the edge. Only the fact that we were too deep for the moonlight to reach us and there were no windows around gave me the barest hold over my wolf side.

I wanted to phase. I wanted to change into a wolf and make the guards, Eileen, Sir Harbrand, Madam Opal, and everyone else who was a member of the Monster Abolition and Eradication Society pay for the lives they had taken and the torture they had done. I was sick of torture. Between Dr. Fagrin, the Demon Knight, the Wiccan Enforcer, Chutka the Shambler, demons who fed on pain and fear, Grayson, and the prejudice I still faced at the Academy for my werewolf heritage, I was fed up with cruelty toward anyone who was different. I made a vow to end the Maes if it was the last thing I did.

My heated inward discussion stopped abruptly at the sight of the man chained to a streetlight pole in the city section.

My dad lay facedown and motionless. I recognized him by the tattered red and white checkered shirt he wore. It was one of his favorites because my mom had given it to him the Christmas before she passed away. He only wore it on special occasions. I wondered if he and Julianne had been heading on a date night before Grayson jumped them. It took all of my power to walk slowly toward him with feigned nonchalance instead of rushing to his side and falling to my knees like I so wanted.

"Is that one of them?" Eileen asked.

She dropped to one knee with her hand on her baton and grabbed Dad's hair. Lifting him up to peer at his face, she nodded. "Yep. That's the male." She released his hair and his face hit the floor.

She looked around. "I wonder what they did with the female."

With a speed that shocked me, Dad leaped up and grabbed Eileen's baton with one hand and her hair with the other. He put the baton to her throat and glared at me.

"Release me," he growled, his voice gruff.

If I hadn't noticed the shirt, I wouldn't have recognized my dad. His gaze was vicious, his hair wild, and the scruff of a beard that had never shown on his carefully groomed face made him look both homeless and wild. He had a black eye and dark bruises showed on the side of his face and his neck. An untreated cut on his brow had dripped blood down his cheek that was now crusted and dry. There was a desperation to his gaze and a weakness to the way his hand shook as it held the baton that made me stare instead of running to him. I was completely frozen to the spot by shock.

"Release me," he commanded again, his voice louder this time.

His words freed me.

"Release him," I said. I hurried toward them.

Eileen tried to shake her head, but Dad held her hair tighter and she let out a squeak of pain.

"Eileen, the keys, now," I commanded.

Dad's eyes focused on me. I watched as recognition warred with fear, and I knew he was worried that his mind was playing tricks on him.

"Finn?"

I ignored him for the moment, afraid that if Eileen found out who I was, she would sound the alarm before we had her under control. She fumbled for the keys tucked into a pouch at her belt and held them out. I tore them from her hand and found the round one that would fit into the manacle around Dad's throat.

"Keep her quiet," I told him.

Dad put a hand over Eileen's mouth. She watched us both with wide eyes.

"Finn, it is you!" he said with such relief I had to fight back tears.

"I'm going to get you out of here," I replied. I managed to get the key into the hole on the back of the manacle and turn it. The manacle opened to reveal the red, raw skin underneath. I swallowed against the anger that tightened my throat and said, "Where's Julianne."

"They took her."

The sorrow in Dad's voice was agonizing. He hung his head dejectedly and his hand slipped from Eileen's mouth. Before she could scream, I grabbed her by the throat and squeezed just hard enough to let her know I meant business. I pushed her against the light pole.

"Where would they take her?" I demanded.

She shook her head. "I don't know." Surprise still showed on her face at my betrayal.

I felt her suck in a breath and tightened my hold. "If you try to call for help, I'll snap your neck."

"Finn!" my dad said in shock behind me.

I kept my gaze on Eileen. "Why would they take someone from the training grounds?"

At my tightening fingers, she said quickly, "They only take creatures from here that are either dead or almost dead."

I was unwilling to accept that Julianne was dead. I asked through gritted teeth, "Where do they take the almost dead?"

"Sir Harbrand has an infirmary," she replied, her voice raspy from my grip. "He does what he can to heal the creatures so they can be targets again."

"Where?" I demanded.

She pointed to a set of doors near the escalator. "But you can't get there without a keycard."

I grabbed her keycard from her belt with my free hand and said, "I have a keycard."

"Hey!" she protested.

I brought my face close to hers. "I could never find anyone attractive who takes pleasure in the pain and torture of others."

I released her neck, but before she could scream for help, I grabbed the gun from her belt and shot her in the chest. At that distance, it must have hurt, but the electricity surging through her body cut off whatever protest she would have made. I waited until she slumped unconscious to the ground, then slipped the baton from her belt as well.

I handed the baton to my dad. His stare at my actions said so much more than words ever could.

"Take it," I barked out when he made no move to accept the baton.

When his hand closed around the stick, I saw the burn marks the trainees' bullets had made on his skin. Eileen's comment about the heart not being able to handle electricity well made me watch him closely. His skin was a sickly gray color and when he straightened, he swayed.

I grabbed his arm to steady him. "Come on, Dad," I said gently. "Let's get you out of here."

"Where are we going?" he asked with confusion in his voice.

"To find Julianne," I replied.

Chapter Five

FROM MY POSITION CROUCHED in the shadows of a fake building in the city district of the training grounds, I counted five guards between us and the doors Eileen had pointed to.

I glanced at my father, but the hope that he would be of any help vanished immediately. He was sitting on the ground with his back against the same building. His knees were pulled up to his chest and he stared at the baton in his hands as though wondering where it had come from. I hoped his confusion and shock would fade with time, but time was the one thing Julianne didn't have.

"Stay here, Dad," I told him. When he didn't acknowledge that I had spoken, I set a hand on his shoulder.

Dad jerked back with wide eyes and the kind of fear on his face that made my heart ache.

"Dad, it's me, Finn."

Dad's fear vanished and he smiled. "It's been a while, Finn."

I nodded. "Too long. I'm going to get Julianne so we can all go home, alright, Dad?"

"Home," he repeated. "Home would be good."

I touched his hand that held the baton. "I need to clear a path to the doors and I want you to stay here. If anyone shows up, stun them with the baton, got it?"

He held up the baton and nodded, his eyes a bit more focused. "I'll stun them with the baton."

"Right," I replied.

I didn't want to leave him there, but if Julianne had any chance, I had to get her away from the Maes. Thoughts of the baby kept swarming my mind, but I pushed them away. One step at a time. I had to know if Julianne was alive first.

I crept from shadow to shadow. The impulse to phase into wolf form was strong, but I knew if I was going to take them down in silence, using the gun was my best bet.

It felt like a game, creeping up on the guards without making a sound. Some instinct inside of me thrummed with pleasure at being the hunter. I could feel my body responding and noticed how softly my feet touched the ground and how soundlessly I even breathed as I approached my prey. It was as though my wolf side found a way to exist within my human side.

I wasn't surprised when the colors of my human vision faded to the grays of the wolf. The musky scent of the guard reached me from a few paces behind him. With a breath, I could tell he had eaten lasagna and garlic bread for dinner. The fact that he had a pet cat at home and that he carpooled with someone who owned a wirehaired terrier was catalogued effortlessly in the back of my mind.

Adrenaline raced through my veins as I closed the last few steps between me and the guard. A single shout or any sound other than Eileen's silenced electric gun would send the hundreds of guards I had seen on the floors above down on our heads. I knew better than to hope my father and I could survive such an onslaught. Any chance we had relied on complete silence.

I let out a soundless breath and lunged at the guard. Before he could make so much as a squeak, I shoved him to the floor and shot his exposed neck with an electric bullet. His back arched as the spider-like legs of the bullet sunk into his skin, then he slumped motionless to the floor.

"One down, four to go," I whispered.

As I crept through the shadows toward the next guard, I told myself I was enjoying it too much. But there was something so fulfilling about stalking my prey, approaching them downwind, and taking them out without a sound. The surprise on the face of the next woman made me smile even as her body convulsed and then stilled in unconsciousness.

I told myself that at least they weren't dead, but the wolf side of me didn't agree. Any enemy to my family was better off dead. A shudder ran through me with the fear of how close I was to losing control. As I pulled down the fourth guard and shot him, I told myself I wouldn't become the monster they feared. The detached side of me noted with irony that I already was. I had been born that way.

I reached the fifth guard in record time. He was the closest to the doors that were our target. I pulled him down and couldn't help grinning when I shot him in the neck, then a voice spoke and shattered my triumph.

"Hey, what are you doing?"

I had shoved the gun in my waistband when I crouched to check the guard. A glance out of the corner of my eye showed two guards who had just entered the training grounds from the escalator. Both had their guns trained on me, but their fingers were at the side of their triggers as if they were uncertain whether I was one of them or the enemy. I chose to take advantage of that uncertainty.

"He fell and I'm just checking—"

I rose before I completed my sentence and slipped my gun from my waistband with a smoothness even Vicken would envy. I pulled the trigger twice before they could react. A bullet struck each in the throat and they fell to the ground. My gaze shifted from their bodies to the sight of my dad leaning against the closest building. His mouth was open and it was too late to hope he hadn't seen everything.

I waited for his words of condemnation, for him to tell me I was a monster and I should get away from him.

Instead, he pushed away from the wall, gave a single nod when he approached me, and said, "It's a good thing I took you out to practice with guns when you were twelve."

I could only stare at him when he passed me by on the way to the doors. There was no way I would tell him about storming the Mythic Labs with both Mercer's guns and the labs' guns and that I went through so many bullets and weapons there was no way to count them. Let him assume my aim had been luck drawn from skills I had learned on one shooting outing four years ago. I would choose that rather than let him know what a monster I really was.

"Where's the keycard?" he asked.

I pulled it wordlessly from my back pocket and handed it to him. He swiped the reader and it gave a ding of approval.

He pulled the door open. "You coming?" he asked.

I glanced back once at the two guards that lay in a heap in the middle of the floor.

"Hold on," I told him.

I grabbed the guards by the straps on their armored vests and pulled them into the shadows with the other one I had downed. On impulse, I also took their guns. I shoved one into the front of my waistband and another in the back, then handed the last one to my dad when I reached the door.

He tossed the baton down and took the gun.

"Let's save your stepmother," he said with a determined glint in his eye that told of his former self returning.

"I'll go first," I told him.

He followed me down the next hallway. The cloying scent of blood and demons was everywhere. I ignored the shadows of demons waiting next to closed glass rooms. Inside, the curtainless rooms contained a bed with a monster tied by restraints to the top. Some monsters were motionless while others fought their restraints and yelled for help. It was only the thought of Julianne in trouble that kept me moving forward.

The sound of talking made my footsteps slow. Dad did the same. We approached the next corridor with bated breaths, our guns ready. When we reached the corner, my heart constricted.

A huge glass-enclosed room to our left contained white-jacketed men and women standing around a table. On the table lay Julianne, motionless, pale, and looking more thin and frail than I had ever seen her. At the head of the table stood a husky-looking man with in a white lab coat. His black hair had been slicked back and a red bandana was tied around his forehead as though he was some sort of doctor rock star. He had a close-cropped black beard and a mustache that turned up at the corners. He was facing us directly; if either Dad or I moved, we would be in plain sight.

"As you can see, her vitals have diminished to the point that sending her back into the training grounds would be a waste. This is why humans aren't good candidates for training, be they mothers of monsters or not."

Several around the table laughed as though they were talking about bugs or pests instead of a mother whose baby had been taken away.

"What do you propose at this point, Sir Harbrand?" a young woman in a white coat asked.

"Termination," the man with the bandana replied simply. "And as soon as her vitals show that she has expired, we'll perform a full autopsy to better understand why a human can carry a werewolf child when no other monster has such capabilities."

"Do we know if the infant's werewolf gene will be active or dormant?" a man with a clipboard asked.

Sir Harbrand shook his head. "Unfortunately, only time will tell." He winked. "Fortunately, we have the time that she doesn't."

Laughter circled the table again. My hand tightened on my gun. I heard Dad mutter a curse he would have scolded me for under different circumstances.

Sir Harbrand nodded at a young man near the machines Julianne was hooked up to. "Edgart, begin the process." He turned to the others who appeared to be his students. "A mild sedative will be injected into her I.V. followed by a lethal dose of pentobarbital. It's a seizure medication that in a large dose like the one Edgart will be administering, will shut down her heart and brain functions."

"No!" Dad shouted.

I shot twice at the glass surrounding the room. I wasn't surprised when the bullets didn't penetrate, but the sound had the desired effect of stopping everyone, including Edgart, and turning their attention to me.

Sir Harbrand didn't seem at all frazzled by our appearance. He walked toward the glass doors with his hands behind his back and a calculating expression on his face. He was at least a foot taller than me and, given the width of his shoulders, I had the impression that he could bench-press a bear. I guess it took strength to keep all of the monsters under his command in control.

"You must be the werewolf," he said. His voice was muffled slightly by the thick glass.

"You must be Sir Fartcan," I replied.

"Harbrand," he corrected mildly.

I ignored him. "Tell your students to back away from the table."

Sir Harbrand gave an amused smile at my command. "You can't reach us in here."

I pulled out Eileen's keycard. "Can't I?"

His eyes widened at the sight of the card. I waved it in front of the reader with a triumphant smile. To my dismay, the reader gave a flat beep.

Sir Harbrand let out an amused laugh. "See? It's our job to erase monsters from the earth lest it be overrun with their stupidity and—"

Whatever he was going to say vanished from his lips at the appearance of a man in a lab coat walking down the hallway with his gaze on a file he carried. I took a cue from Harbrand's expression and fired without giving the man a chance to react.

"Check his coat," I told Dad who was already on his way over to the fallen form.

Dad pulled out a keycard and held it up with a triumphant laugh. "We got it!"

"Don't you dare," Sir Harbrand threatened when Dad reached my side. He handed me the card. I waved it in front of the reader while keeping my gaze on those in the room.

An approving ding sounded. Sir Harbrand and I stared at each other for a brief second. I put my hand on the door. He backed off several steps and then ran. Chaos ensued inside the glass room. The students scrambled over one another to get away from the table. But the door we used appeared to be the only escape.

Calls of, "Mad werewolf!" and "We're under attack!" rang out.

Someone bumped Julianne's table. The smallest whimper of pain escaped from her.

"Freeze!" I shouted. My voice reverberated off the glass with the force of the shout. The students and Sir Harbrand stopped moving. Everyone turned around slowly as if certain they would be the one shot.

At my nod, Dad ran to the table. He quickly unhooked Julianne's I.V. and gathered her into his arms. Any doubt I had that he was able to carry her given his condition faded at the protective look on his face. He would carry her to the ends of the earth if he had to.

I aimed my gun at Harbrand. "It's a pity this gun doesn't have real bullets. Someone like you should pay for the suffering you've inflicted on others." I squeezed the trigger and the bullet struck the center of his chest. He fell writhing to the floor. I shifted my gaze to the others. They backed away at the intensity of my stare. "And to the rest of you, know that I will be coming for anyone who approves of and is involved with the torture of any creature, be it monster or human." I lowered my voice to a threatening level. "If you stay with the Maes, I will hunt each of you down individually and see that you undergo the same tortures you have inflicted on the monsters here. I would recommend sleeping with one eye open from now on."

"Let's go," Dad commanded from the door.

I fired several shots into the crowd before I left. I might not have enough bullets to shoot all of them, but those who were hit might hesitate to inflict such pain on others after they recovered.

I slammed a fist into the inside card reader before I left. The reader shattered and sparks flew up from the attachments beneath it. When I shut the door, I pulled on it, but it refused to open. I gave a grim smile at the thought that only a card from the outside would release the students and their fallen teacher of torment.

Dad was already halfway up the hall. I was almost to him when a form caught the corner of my eye. I turned to see a woman lying motionless on a bed. Something about her profile kept my attention. I slowed my steps and approached the door. The closer I got, the more certain I became that I was looking at someone from Vicken's lineage.

I pushed the door, but it refused to open. I pulled the new card from my pocket and used it on the reader. The machine beeped and I heard the door lock release. With my heart thundering in my chest, I crossed the floor toward the bed. The woman's cheekbones stood out in sharp contrast to her pale skin; her aquiline nose and tightly pressed lips reminded me of my friend. I glanced at the band around her wrist. The printed name 'Donessa Ruvine' made my heart leap into my throat.

"Finn, what you doing? We've got to go!" Dad insisted from the door of the room.

"This is Vicken's mother," I replied.

Dad looked from me to the unconscious woman. He let out a breath and stepped into the room. "Right. What do we do?"

"She needs blood," I said. I looked around for something I could use to cut myself. My eyes landed on a set of drawers against the wall. I pulled open the first one and was rewarded with an entire drawer filled with plastic-wrapped scalpels. I held one up. "This'll do."

I hurried back to the bed and had pressed the knife to the place just below Sparrow's name on my wrist when my dad caught my hand. I glanced over to see Julianne resting curled up on her side where Dad had set her gently on the floor.

"She needs blood," I repeated.

He held out his hand. "If anyone's giving her blood, it's me."

I stared at him. "Dad, it'll make you sick."

"Would it make you sick?"

He watched me closely as I thought about my answer. "Well, yes," I replied.

He opened his hand again. "Give it to me. You need to stay strong if we're getting out of this."

I couldn't help my surprise when I asked, "Why? Shouldn't you be the strong one?"

He shook his head. "I need you to come back for your baby sister."

My mouth fell open. "Baby sister," I repeated.

Dad nodded. In the place of the terrified, feral man I had found in the training grounds stood my father, calm, confident, and able to see the situation for what it was.

"I need to get Julianne to a hospital as fast as I can. It's the only hope she has. You need to come back here and bring your baby sister home." He looked through the glass walls and a hint of desperation surfaced in his gaze. "I don't know how, but you've got to do it." His gaze locked back on me. "You're the only one who can."

I nodded because it felt like the only thing I could do. "I'll do it. I promise."

He nodded. "Good boy. Now let's get this vampire up."

He pressed the knife to the vein at the base of his thumb. I heard his swift intake of breath just before blood welled from the wound. Without waiting for me to tell him what to do, he held his hand over the vampire's mouth. I heard the minute splash as the first drop of blood fell onto her lips.

"She's not moving," Dad said. He squeezed his hand and more blood dripped down.

I saw the Donessa's eyes move beneath her eye lids. "It's working," I whispered.

With a speed I should have expected but still startled me anyway, the Donessa's head lunged forward and she bit Dad's hand with her fangs.

Dad gave a startled yelp, but held still as she drank his blood.

I watched his face pale. "That's not a sensation you want to experience every day," he said, his voice level. He glanced at the straps that held her wrists. "Should we untie her?"

I shook my head. "Not yet."

I watched her take several more deep gulps, then said, "Donessa Ruvine, you need to stop now."

She didn't. I wasn't surprise. Both of the times I had given blood to Vicken, he had been at a point where being rational wasn't an option. For any creature on the edge of death, survival was of the utmost importance, and by the looks of things, the Donessa had been on her way out of this life.

I put a hand on her upper arm. "Donessa Ruvine, you need to stop drinking now," I said in a slightly louder voice.

Dad held his arm and I could see the fingers of his other hand begin to shake. I whispered, "Vicken, please forgive me." I leaned over the bed and shouted, "Donessa Ruvine. Stop. Now!"

Her eyes flew open. Yellow irises peered up at me, then shifted to Dad. Her eyes widened and she opened her mouth enough to withdraw her fangs from Dad's wrist. He backed away. Without breaking my gaze from the vampire's, I handed him one of the rolls of gauze I had found in a drawer.

"Wrap it up. You don't want to bleed in front of a vampire. Trust me."

The Donessa's eyes narrowed. "Do I know you?"

I shook my head. "No, but I go to school with your son. My name's Finn Briscoe. Vicken sent me to get you out."

"Vicken?" she repeated. Her eyes filled with tears; when she blinked, they flowed down the sides of her pale face. "Is he safe?"

I lied to her because she was in no shape to take the truth. "Yes, he's fine. We've got to get you out of here."

Certain that my father and I were no longer at the risk of being drained dry by the Donessa, I undid her straps. As soon as her hands were free, she sat up and broke the bonds on her feet. With a fluidity of movement despite her weakness, the Donessa led the way to the door. Dad bent to pick up Julianne, but I beat him to it.

"Reserve your strength; we're going to need it," I told him quietly when I picked Julianne up in my arms.

"What happened to her?" Donessa Ruvine asked.

My dad's voice was flat when he replied, "Sir Harbrand."

The vampire's lips pulled back from her teeth in a terrifying grimace. "If we run into him on the way out…." She left the sentence hanging.

"He's stuck for the moment," I replied. "I shot him and left him locked in one of his operating rooms."

Dad gave me a triumphant look. The sight of his black eye and bruised face made me wish I had done far more than just shoot the man.

"Good," the Donessa replied. She peered down the hall, then glanced back at us. "How are we getting out of here?"

I gave an embarrassed shrug. "We're sort of winging it at this point."

She nodded. "Fair enough. Let's go."

Chapter Six

THE DONESSA TURNED OUT to be a very valuable ally. She had no problem ranging ahead to see where the guards were. The glass walls gave us little the hide behind, but with the vampire's excellent eyesight, she saw them and directed us down different paths before we were spotted.

The sound of a siren reached my ears. I slowed.

"What's wrong?" my dad asked. His face was pale and I could see the sweat standing out on his skin. He was already feeling the effects of being bitten by the vampire, but he refused any assistance.

"Sirens. They're onto us," I replied.

The Donessa nodded. "Good. Change of plans. I thought we could make it out through the original garage, but instead, we're going out the way you came in."

I couldn't help my shock. "But it's heavily guarded."

"I'll bet it's not right now," she replied.

We burst through the doors near the escalator just as the sound of footsteps rang down. The Donessa grabbed my arm and pulled me into the shadows beneath the escalator before they stormed by. My dad leaned with his hands on his knees, his breath coming in gasps. I shifted Julianne so that her head rested against my shoulder. The sound of her heart was faint.

"We need to hurry," I whispered as soon as the guards disappeared through the infirmary doors. "She doesn't have long and he doesn't look good."

"Why are you three here?" the vampire asked with suspicion in her yellow eyes.

I went with the truth because the Donessa would find out from her husband if we ever got out of the restructured mall.

"I'm a werewolf. They took my dad and stepmom in the hopes of getting a werewolf to study, but Dad's genes are dormant and Julianne is human."

The Donessa studied me. For a moment, it looked as though she was weighing leaving us behind. I was struck by the coldness of the vampire's gaze. The look in her eyes was one I had only seen once on her son's face, and that was when he nearly beat me to death during my first days at Haunted High. At least I knew where he got his prejudice against werewolves.

"You saved my life," she said finally. "I wouldn't expect that from one of your kind."

I thought my dad would argue against her words the way he had when Don Ruvine had shown the same kind of prejudice at the Academy. When he didn't, a glance in his direction showed that his condition was rapidly declining. He had sunk to the ground. Sweat stained his tattered shirt and he eyes were fever bright. He looked up at me without appearing to see me.

"Dad?" I asked.

"It's the bite," the Donessa replied levelly. "It does that to a human."

The thought that her bite might affect him more powerfully than me hadn't occurred to me. "Is he going to be alright?" I asked.

She shook her head. "Not without fluids. He needs to get to a hospital." She paused, then said as though she forced it, "Or one of our infirmaries."

I knew she referred to the mansions that were the vampires' lair. Each was fully stocked with staff and a complete infirmary ready to deal with a multitude of inflictions. I made myself ask, "Will you take them there?"

She let out a breath as if saying the words hurt, "I might take them. But not you."

I fought back the urge to bristle at the accusation in her tone. "I don't need to go," I told her. "Just save them. I need to stay here. They have my baby sister somewhere in this place. I've got to find her."

She looked at Julianne. "That makes sense. Your stepmother smells of blood."

I knew by the pallor of her skin that the vampire hadn't drank enough blood to fill what was lost. Even running to the escalator had cost her. She needed blood as much as Julianne and my dad needed help. Getting all three of them out of the Maes headquarters was the only way to save them.

I turned so that the vampire had to look at me instead of Julianne. "I saved your life by getting you out. Do you promise to take my parents to one of your mansions and care for them until they can go home?" I knew better than to say until I came for them. We would be lucky to leave the headquarters once; I didn't dare hope I would escape a second time, but I had to try for my sister's sake.

She looked annoyed at being put on the spot, but I wasn't about to move until she gave me her reassurance.

The Donessa finally nodded. "You have my word."

Relief filled me. Before she could react, I set Julianne in her arms and pulled out my guns. "I'm going to make a phone call. Stay with them."

I was about to use my keycard at the door of the escalator when a thought occurred to me. I slipped around the other side where I had hidden the three guards I had felled before we entered the infirmary. I took the armored vest from one, a gun belt from another, and kicked off my shoes to pull on the heavy work boots of the last one. Fortunately, his feet were only a size bigger than mine. With my dark shirt and the guns back in their holsters, I hoped I could pass off as one of the guards.

All three had cellphones in their pockets, but none of them had reception in the basement of the mall. I took the three phones in the hopes that at least one wasn't locked and left the unconscious men behind. Knowing I couldn't delay any longer, I used the keycard on the door and stepped onto the escalator. I glanced up and my heart slowed. At least a dozen other guards were heading down.

I kept my face averted and pretended to be busy checking the slide on my gun mostly so I could have it in my hand in case any of them grew suspicious.

"What's the status?" the first one who passed me asked.

I cleared my throat and replied, "There's a firefight in the infirmary. They need backup."

The others began to jog down until the one in front held up a hand. "Then why aren't you down there?" he shouted back up at me.

I swallowed and thought quickly. "They sent me to get help. There's monsters everywhere. Be ready. I'll be back with others."

He nodded and continued down. I was grateful he didn't think to point out the fact that they were the backup.

I reached the regular parking garage and searched the area. Fortunately, Donessa Ruvine was right. With the guards all heading to the infirmary, the place was empty.

I held up the first phone, but there were no bars. The second was protected by a password and wouldn't open to the main screen. When I swiped the screen on the third, I let out a sigh of relief. It showed the main screen and one bar. I punched the number quickly.

"Hello?" Drake's voice was uncertain.

"Drake, put Dara on the phone."

"Finn, I thought I'd never hear your voice again!" my brother said. "Are you okay? Did you find Dad and Julianne?"

"I don't have time to explain. Put Dara on the phone," I demanded. In the moments between, I felt bad for the way I had spoken to him, but now wasn't the time to make it up.

Dara finally answered. "Finn, what's going on?"

"Dara, I need you to call Don Ruvine, Vicken's father, and have him trace this number to get our location. Get his number from the Academy. We're going to be in serious trouble in just a minute."

"Finn, what's happening there?" she asked with worry in her voice.

I thought of the displays, Madam Opal, and the training grounds. "I don't know where to start. We're going to have to talk later. But Julianne, my dad, and Donessa Ruvine are in serious trouble if they don't get help soon. I just hope he has the resources to get them out of here." A noise sounded up the escalator. "I've got to go. Tell them to get here right away."

I hung up just as several more guards appeared at the top of the escalator. I started up as they jogged down.

"Hurry!" I told them. "The fighting's in the infirmary. I'll bring more backup!"

"Right," their leader said. At his command, their jog turned into a mad dash down the stairs.

I reached the main floor of the mall and glanced around. I needed something that would help me get Dad, Julianne, and the Donessa out of the mall quickly, but I didn't know what that could be. By the sound of things, more guards were being mustered on the floor above. If they tried to stop our escape, we would be in serious trouble. I had to find a faster mode of travel than running. My eyes fell on a cart near one of the barred enclosures. It looked like the type used for maintenance or carrying supplies.

I ran over to it and maneuvered the cart to the side of the escalator. It was surprisingly fast for a vehicle used to deliver food and jugs of water to the display occupants. I parked the cart and got out, then on impulse, I took the key. I didn't want anyone moving it when I went down below.

"You there!" a voice shouted.

My heart skipped a beat. I looked up to see guards running toward me. I reached slowly behind me for the gun hidden at the back of my belt. I hoped if they didn't see me go for the one in my holster, they might think I wasn't trying to fight back. My hand closed around the cold grip. I sucked in a tight breath, ready to take as many of them down with me as I could.

"Fall in line!" the leader barked at me.

I looked from the cart to the guards who slowed to a stop near the top of the escalator.

"Uh, yes sir!" I replied.

I jogged to the back of the group. As soon as I joined, the leader shouted, "Move it!"

We ran down the stairs in a tight pack. I fought back the urge to smile like a maniac with the way my heart thundered in my chest and adrenaline pounded through my veins. We reached the parking garage and ran to the next set of escalators. I made sure to hang at the back on the way down. When we made it to the training grounds, the leader turned without hesitation toward the infirmary. I jogged with them several steps, then fell back at the last minute and ducked beneath the escalator.

A hand grabbed my shoulder and slammed me to the ground. I found myself staring up into the bright, hungry eyes of Vicken's mother.

"It's me, Finn!" I said before she could pull the trigger of the gun she aimed at my head.

"Finn," I heard Dad say weakly.

The Donessa lowered the weapon. "You changed clothes," she said flatly.

I nodded. "I needed to blend in. It worked. We've got to go now before it's too late."

"We're not going to get far," the Donessa replied. "Your stepmother isn't doing well and your father, either." She didn't have to say that her strength was faltering. I could tell just by looking at her.

I would have offered her blood, but my dad's warning that I would need my strength to come back for my baby sister lingered in my mind. Instead, I bent and picked Julianne up before the vampire tried to carry her. My stepmother let out a small gasp of pain and clung to me.

"I've got you," I reassured her gently. "Just hold on." My dad tried to rise, but his legs shook and he fell back to his knees. The sight of both of them in such poor condition made my chest hurt. I forced my emotions aside and grabbed his arm, hefting it over my shoulder. "Come on, Dad. One last push," I told him.

"One last push," he mumbled as he rose wearily at my side. "We've got this."

"Yes, we do," I agreed. I glanced over my shoulder at the Donessa. "Ready?"

She shook her head. "But if we don't move now, we might not ever again."

Her words echoed in my head as we crept around to the front of the escalator. The card reader beeped and the doors slid open. We crouched on the stairs and let the escalator carry us up. I breathed a sigh of relief at the empty parking garage.

"One more escalator and we're home free," I told them.

Donessa Ruvine and my dad followed me with slow steps to the next escalator. I watched the top as we rode up, ready to grab my gun if any guards appeared. Fortunately, none did. It looked as though our luck would hold out. If we could just make it to the cart, we would be home free.

As soon as my head cleared the top of the escalator, my heart fell. Guards lined the exit four deep. Their guns were out and their eyes were trained on me.

"Valiant effort, Mr. Briscoe."

Madam Opal stood to the side of the men and women who needed only her word to shoot. Behind her waited the other members of the Maes leadership. The looks of disapproval on their faces were clear.

I pulled the key from my pocket and passed it back to Donessa Ruvine before our hands were visible.

"Get my dad in the cart," I whispered.

I stepped off the escalator and grinned at Madam Opal, then shrugged, which wasn't easy with Julianne in my arms. "I had to try, right?"

"I'll give you that," Madam Opal replied. "But we weren't fooled."

I laughed at that. "You know you just accepted a werewolf into the Society, right? Is that because you weren't fooled?"

Her eyes narrowed and I saw several of the other leadership members mutter to each other. From the corner of my eye, I watched the Donessa slowly help my dad into the cart.

"You'll suffer for your disrespect," Madam Opal warned.

I glared at her. "You know all about suffering, don't you? You seem to have made an art form of helping other people suffer here."

"People?" Madam Opal scoffed. "You mean monsters."

"Ready," Donessa Ruvine whispered from behind me and to my right.

"I mean people," I shot back at the leader of the Maes. "Living, breathing people with hopes and dreams just like you." I made a show of looking around and took several steps backwards toward the cart until I felt it with the backs of my legs. "Or maybe not like you. I hope they're not like you. One Madam Opal is too many for this world."

Her gun was out of her holster and in her hand the moment my words left my mouth.

"Be careful what you say, Mr. Briscoe. These bullets aren't your little electric shock. They'll kill you as sure as you're standing there."

"You won't do that," I replied, though my blood ran cold at the thought.

"And why won't I?" she challenged. She lifted her gun so that it was pointing at my head.

"You want me for your display," I replied. I walked slowly around to the side of the cart and handed Julianne to

Donessa Ruvine. The vampire set her gently on the front seat.

When I looked back, Madam Opal was walking toward me. Her eyes moved from the cart and then back to my face.

I spoke to keep her distracted. "If you shoot me, you'll lose probably the only Alpha werewolf you're ever going to have."

Greed showed in her eyes at my words and her gun lowered slightly. It was the opening I was waiting for.

I jumped into the driver's seat of the cart and turned the key the Donessa had left in the ignition. The moment the motor hummed to life, I stepped on the gas. The cart's wheels squealed on the tiled floor as it sped toward the guards.

"Vicken?"

I turned my head at the Donessa's voice. Following her gaze, I spotted Vicken in one of the caged rooms. He was watching everything with wide eyes, his hands on the bars and his expression pained. When he met my gaze, he yelled, "Finn!" and hit the bar with his fist, trying to break free. I saw his knuckles split with the force of the blow, but the bars didn't show any sign of breaking.

"Vicken!" the Donessa said. "We need to get him!"

Vicken's gaze shifted to his mother and his eyes widened. "Go!" he shouted, looking back at me. "Get her out of there!"

"I'll come back for you; I promise!" I shouted. The sight of my friend trapped behind the bars filled me with rage. I wanted to break him out, but there was no time.

"Look out!" Dad warned from behind me.

We were heading straight for Madam Opal's guard, but I didn't swerve. I wanted to go out the main doors and they had made the mistake of standing right in front of them.

I gritted my teeth and kept my foot pressed to the floor. Shots were fired in our direction. I leaned over Julianne to protect her.

"Stop them!" Madam Opal shouted.

More shots sounded. Several hit the sides of the cart and others whizzed over our heads. Most of the guards leaped out of the way at the last second. One, a stalwart looking man with steel in his gaze, planted his feet and aimed his gun right at Julianne. I knew there was no way she would be able to survive an electric bullet.

"Hold on!" I called to Dad and the Donessa.

I leaned over Julianne as the man pulled the trigger. Any hope I had that the bullet would hit my vest vanished when it latched onto my upper arm. I had a brief sense of satisfaction when the guard who shot me was hit by the cart and bounced off to the side, then the legs of the bullet sunk into my skin and the electricity surged.

I jerked back in my seat as the jolts raced over my body and through my muscles. My jaw locked and my hands and feet refused to work through the agony. I watched in horror as the glass doors to the converted mall loomed closer. Huge metal plates slid down, no doubt part of Madam Opal's security defense, but I had no way to swerve. The last of the guards leaped free before we reached them. I had no idea if we would clear the plate in time. I wanted to swerve, to cover Julianne, to do anything but watch the doors race toward us. I couldn't pull my foot from the gas. It was going to be close.

The cart hit the doors so hard they shattered. I felt the shards cut my face and hands, and then we were through. The cart bounced down the shallow steps, jumped over the curb, and then was racing through the parking lot.

"Stop us, Finn!" the Donessa said.

But the paralysis refused to let up. I couldn't say why I was still conscious. I could only stare as the wall on the far side of the parking lot came closer and closer. We were going to slam into it and there was nothing I could do about it. I couldn't even close my eyes. I wanted to apologize to the others in the cart for getting them out of one danger only to place them in the way of another, but I wasn't even able to do that. I had killed us all.

Shots rang out and small explosions happened beneath the cart all at the same time. The vehicle slowed. Forms ghosted to either side of us.

"Stop the cart," a man yelled.

I blinked and recognized Don Ruvine running far faster than any human or wolf ever had.

"He can't," the Donessa called from the back seat. "He's been shot!"

The Don glanced over my shoulder and his eyes widened. He grabbed my foot and moved it off the gas pedal. The cart stopped almost immediately.

"Celia?" he whispered reverently.

"Victor," she replied with relief in her voice.

Tears streamed down the Don's cheeks when he reached for his wife.

"I never thought…." He let the words fade away.

"I know," she replied. She sniffed, then I saw her straighten. "The werewolves need help. And Vicken's still in there! We need to help him!"

"We can't right now," the Don told her. "They've closed their shield plates; there's no way through." His voice lowered. "Given the amount of guards our scans showed, that might be a blessing. We don't have enough people to fight our way inside. Until you crashed through that door, I didn't know how we were going to get you out." He paused, then said, "Celia?"

"Blood," she replied in a weak voice.

"Get the helicopter!" the Don commanded. "Load them all in! Now!"

I wanted to protest. My baby sister was still there and the expression on Vicken's face remained burned in my mind as he watched me leave with his mother on the cart. But I couldn't do more than sit there locked in agony. They lifted me into the belly of the helicopter. My last sight was of the mall, its many windows covered by metal plates that sealed me away from the chance of rescuing the two who needed it most. A hand touched my arm and the pain faded into darkness.

Chapter Seven

I WOKE UP IN a dim room. The quiet beeping of the monitor by my head told me that we had made it to Don and Donessa Ruvine's mansion. The memories of what had transpired pushed against me with such urgency I couldn't rest any longer. I sat up, unplugged the monitor so it wouldn't sound an alarm, then pulled the sticky pads from my chest and back. A glance at my arm showed faint burn marks where the electric bullet had hit. I felt a pang of guilt for how quickly it was healing compared to those I had seen on my dad and Julianne.

The thought of my parents brought me to my feet. The shoes I had taken from the guard were gone, as well as the vest. My dark shirt had been replaced with a white tee-shirt. I also wore simple drawstring sweatpants. I shied away from thinking about that; the idea that someone else had changed my clothes wasn't a welcome one.

I slipped from the room and walked silently up the hall. The marble floor felt cold beneath my bare feet. I followed my nose down another quiet hallway. The realization that I was using scent to track down my parents made me smile. Being a werewolf definitely had its perks. But my smile faded away completely at the thought that they were in this situation because I was a werewolf.

The sound of beeping from the room where Dad and Julianne's scent was the strongest made my footsteps slow. I hesitated by the door. Seeing my dad the way he had been in the training grounds had been harder than I could have imagined. Beaten, fighting for his life, and desperate to protect Julianne, had turned him into something far different from the high school science teacher who wore his lucky tie on test days and who made us ice cream sundaes on Sunday because he said it was meant to be.

I forced myself to step into the dim room and waited for the grays to take over my normal eyesight. The darkness faded and the grays brought everything out in stark contrast. My heart gave a loud beat at the sight of Dad and Julianne.

The vampires had pushed their beds together. As much as they hated werewolves, it touched me to see that simple act of kindness. Dad was asleep on his side, his bruised face painful looking and dark in contrast to the white pillowcase on which he slept. An I.V. had been put in one arm and clear liquid flowed from the bag that hung near the bed. With his other hand, he held Julianne's, his arm looped around her protectively as they slept.

Julianne looked pale and worn. Her I.V.s contained both the clear liquid and a bag of blood. I wondered how she had managed to survive at the Maes headquarters after having her baby there. They definitely hadn't giving her the medical attention she deserved. The fact that she was away from that horrid place made me even more determined to go back and get the others out. Nobody deserved such torture.

"Finn?" she asked softly.

I crossed quickly to her side.

"I'm here, Julianne," I whispered so I didn't wake up Dad. I knelt by the side of the bed so I would be at my stepmom's eye level.

She lifted her hand with the I.V. and set it gently on my cheek. "You're so brave," she whispered. Tears filled her eyes.

I fought back tears of my own and shook my head. "I'm not. It's my fault you were there."

She gave a motherly smile; the tears fell softly down her cheeks and were lost in her blonde hair. "It's not your fault there are bad things that happen in this world, Finn. You take so much on your shoulders. I just want you to know how proud I am of you and how proud I know your mother is. You're so selfless."

I held her hand to my cheek for a moment to remind myself that not everything in this world was out to kill me. It helped to calm the wolf that fought beneath my skin to tear apart those who had hurt my family. At her caring touch, the wolf stilled enough that I could just feel human for that moment.

"Julianne, I'm going back."

Her green eyes widened and she shook her head. "Don't go back, Finn. It's too dangerous."

"I need to save the baby," I told her. "And I need to rescue Vicken. He's the reason I was able to get you out. I can't leave him there."

At the mention of the baby, more tears followed the trail the others had made. It made my heart ache to see the sorrow in her eyes.

"Do what you can," she finally said. "But come back to us safe, okay?"

I nodded. "I will."

I stood and had taken several steps toward the door when she whispered my name again. "Finnley?"

When I turned, she said, "You baby sister's name is Amelia."

"That's a beautiful name," I whispered with a smile.

She sighed and closed her eyes again. "Be careful, Finn," she said.

I nodded even though she couldn't see me and slipped out of the door.

I leaned against the wall and let my head fall to my chest. The baby had a name. The fact made it hard to breathe, it made it real, it brought to the forefront the thought that my baby sister, little Amelia, was in the care of people who had tortured Dad and Julianne. They were the monsters. They were the ones who would take a newborn baby from her mother with the goal of waiting to see if the child would someday turn out to be a werewolf. It was cruel and made me sick. I would save Amelia if it was the last thing I did.

"Finn?"

The familiarity of the voice felt like a balm to my battered soul. "Dara?"

I looked up to see her standing at the end of the hall. She was the last person I had expected to find at the vampire mansion, but the sight of her made me happier than I had words for. "Why are you here?" I asked as I walked toward her.

She closed the distance between us. "When I called Don Ruvine, I made him promise to bring me with them. I was on the helicopter when you crashed out of that place." She shook her head. "I was so worried about you." She stopped about a foot away and looked me up and down. "Are you alright?"

"I'm fine, but I've got to go back," I told her.

The denial on her face was stark. She shook her head, her ashen hair swaying. "You can't go."

"I have to," I told her. "I need to find my baby sister and get Vicken out of there. I can't leave him after he sacrificed himself to save my parents."

Dara nodded resolutely. "Then I'm coming with you."

I shook my head immediately. "There's no way I'm letting you near that place."

She crossed her arms. "Finn, you're going back to the Maes headquarters where they probably want you dead for what you've done. There's no way I'm letting you go alone."

I couldn't help admitting that she was right. It would be nice to have someone along to help, especially since I needed to rescue two people. It was a long shot already and another person might be what I need to make a difference.

I caught myself and shot Dara a glare. "Don't use your empath skills to try to sway me."

She uncrossed her arms. "Fine. But you need me. Who's going to get you away from there once you get them out? If you're hoping Vicken can drive, he won't be able to if he's in the same condition as your parents or you when you came out."

I wanted to refuse, especially since I was thinking clearly with her no longer pushing emotions at me, but she had a point. I watched her closely. "If I let you come, do you promise to stay in the vehicle and away from the Maes until we get out?"

She nodded and I could feel her relief. "I promise."

"Fine," I gave in. "You can come. I need a driver."

She followed me back down the hall. I could hear the triumph in her voice when she said, "You need an army, not a driver, but I'll have to do." She paused, then pointed out, "But you should probably wear shoes."

I glanced down at my feet. "Oh, yeah. I guess I should. Any idea where they put the ones I was wearing when they brought me here?"

"I put them away," Dara replied, emphasizing the *I*.

I paused with my hand on the door to the room where I had come from. "You undressed me?" I asked.

Dara blushed and lowered her gaze. "They were busy with your parents and the Donessa. Someone had to take care of you."

I didn't know how I felt about the fact that it was her. I cleared my throat uncomfortably, but couldn't think of what to say.

Dara looked equally as uncomfortable. "Your, um, hand is healing up."

I glanced down at it in surprise. I hadn't thought about the burn on my palm from the demon fire for quite some time. To my amazement, the skin across my hand was actually a healing pink color instead of the nasty black and red it had been before.

"Dr. Six would be thrilled about that," I said with relief that we had something else to talk about other than me without clothes on. "She didn't think it would ever heal." I opened and closed my hand. The fact that I could do it without pain was incredible.

"I'm glad it's almost gone. That was a scary day," Dara said.

She pulled the guard's shoes from a drawer in the corner and handed them to me.

I smiled at the pair of socks she had rolled up and put inside. "Thanks." I thought about her words and said, "That was the first time we faced a demon. If only we'd known what came next."

She gave a little laugh. "We would've thought we were crazy. Who knew we'd get so used to fighting them."

I gave her a wide-eyed stare. "Are you used to fighting them?"

She nodded, then grinned and shook her head. "I'm lying. I'd be happy if I never saw a demon again."

"Me too," I replied. A thought struck me as I tied my shoe laces. "There are demons all over the Maes headquarters. What if the last piece of Chutka's heart is there?"

Dara gave a wistful smile. "The chance to put the three pieces together and destroy them sounds too good to be true. It could end all of this."

"At least the demon part," I replied. "But the Maes are different." I stood up. "They're pure hatred, you know? They study monsters to find better ways to kill them. It's sick, and there's so many of them. With the Maes out there, how is any monster supposed to be safe?"

"We have the Academy," Dara replied as she led the way up the hall. She gave me a shy look. "And each other."

My heart gave a funny little backflip at the look in her eyes. I couldn't say what drove me to do it, but I took her arm and pulled her gently to me. Before she could protest, I kissed her there in the quiet hallway of the vampire mansion. When I stepped back, my heart was pounding harder than if I had run from a thousand Maes' guards or battled a thousand demons.

She put her fingers to her lips with a smile. "What was that for?"

I smiled back. "I couldn't help it."

She held out her hand. My heart warmed when I took her hand in mine and our fingers linked. We walked that way to a door Dara seemed familiar with. When she let go of my hand to open it, I immediately missed the feeling of her fingers entwined with mine.

At her gesture, I followed her into the dark room.

"What are we doing here?" I whispered. The scent of car exhaust, gasoline, and rubber made it obvious where we were.

"We're going to steal a car," she whispered back, leading me down a short set of stairs.

"Steal a—"

My words were cut short when the lights flipped on to reveal rows upon rows of every vehicle imaginable. When my gaze shifted, I blinked and took a step back at the sight of Don Ruvine watching us from the steps. He had never been a fan of mine, and the fact that I was responsible for his son's captivity with the Maes wasn't lost on me.

"Your plan is to steal a car?" the Don asked. His haughty voice and emotionless expression gave me no idea how he felt about it.

"I think borrow is the term we're going for, right Finn?" Dara replied nervously.

"Uh, yes. We'll definitely return it, we're just—"

"Running away?" the Don suggested as he stalked down the stairs toward us.

I bristled at the accusation in his tone. "No. I wouldn't—"

"Let me remind you, Mr. Briscoe, that vampires are as quick to hold grudges as it is said werewolves are to turn tail and run." I opened my mouth to argue, but he lifted a hand. "However, I can admit that our sayings may be a bit prejudice against your kind."

I watched him with uncertainty. "We weren't ever going to run, sir."

He nodded. "I know." He held out a hand to reveal a single key fob. "I also know where you intend to go."

I glanced at Dara. She looked as surprised as I felt.

"Be careful, Finn. My people aren't warriors. I don't have the resources to send my coven charging headfirst into a place like the Maes' headquarters, but I want to. If I wasn't needed here to care for my wife, I would be the one going instead of you." He gave me the first small, grateful smile I had ever seen on Vicken's father's face. "Though somehow, I feel like you might have a better chance. Promise me you'll take care. People who are cruel are also unpredictable because their acts of cruelty come from something deep and twisted inside. Look for the imbalance and use it against them. Fight fear with fear." He handed me the key fob.

I took it while trying to keep the amazement from my face. "Thank you, sir. I'll do my best."

"I know you will," he replied. "And your family will be given the utmost care until you return."

"Thank you," I told him gratefully.

He left back up the stairs without another word and shut the door to leave us staring after him.

"That was unexpected," Dara said quietly.

I kept my eyes on the door for another moment before I turned away. "He loves his son. They're anxious to see Vicken return."

"We all are," Dara replied. She gave me a knowing look. "It hurt you to hand him over to them."

I nodded and lowered my gaze. "It was the worst thing I've ever done. How could I do that to my friend?" I gritted my teeth. "You didn't see what they do in there. It's sick." I couldn't help the way my shoulders slumped. "I'm tired of seeing all that's messed up with this world. Before I found out I was a werewolf, my biggest worries were my next track meet and bringing up the courage to ask a girl to the high school dance."

Dara waited until I looked back at her. Her violet eyes searched mine when she asked, "Do you regret being a werewolf?"

I forced myself to really think about it. "I hate that me being a werewolf has put so many people in danger, including my family. I hate that every step I take at the Academy is watched with suspicion because of what I am, and I hate the prejudice everywhere we go." I took a calming breath and shook my head. "But I don't hate being a werewolf." I held her gaze. "I love it. I love running in wolf form through the forest, I love being able to smell you before you step into a room."

"That's weird," she said with a half-smile.

I continued, "And I love the way I feel right now with you, as if you complete some part of me I never knew was missing. My dad said werewolves fall in love with their entire heart. Humans hold back because they're afraid to get hurt, but werewolves dive in headlong without questioning whether it's smart or not. They fall in love with their heart, mind, and soul." I smiled at her. "Dara, I'm hopelessly yours. I hope that's okay."

A little laugh escaped her as she watched me, but it was a laugh of joy that touched her violet eyes and made her glow with her smile. She stepped closer to me and looked up into my eyes. "Finn, I'm hopelessly yours, too." She slid her hands into my tangled black hair. "But it scares me," she said before she kissed me.

I closed my eyes and lost myself in the feeling of her lips against mine. When she stepped back, the meaning of her words finally became clear. "Why does it scare you?" I whispered.

Her eyebrows pulled together and the look in her eyes was one of such emotion it was hard for me to breathe. "Because you run towards danger, Finn. You're an Alpha fighting to protect this pack you've made, and it's a dangerous job. I just don't want to see you get hurt."

I swallowed against the tightness of my throat and said, "The only thing that would hurt me is to see you in danger. Promise me you'll stay out of this."

She nodded. "I promise, for you."

I took a steeling breath. "Alright. Let's see what kind of vehicle we have to work with."

I clicked the key fob, expecting one of the little town cars or maybe a small truck to honk in response. Instead, a huge SWAT-looking vehicle at the far end honked and flashed its lights. Dara and I looked at each other. A smile stole across my lips. At least this would be fun.

I drove the midnight black SUV far faster than I probably should have, but with its thick cattle guard, triple set of lights, and all-terrain tires, it was easy to feel invincible as we barreled our way back to the renovated mall. Dara's hand rested in mine, and for a time it was easy to pretend that we were just a couple of teenagers on a road trip with no set destination in mind.

When the rising sun illuminated the outline of the Maes' headquarters, I felt Dara's hand tremble in mine. My muscles tightened and I had to remind myself to breathe. I pulled slowly to the edge of the parking lot and watched the metal-covered windows.

"What's your plan?" Dara asked. I wondered if she kept her voice quiet to hide the fear she felt.

I forced bravado into my tone when I replied, "You're not going to like it."

Her eyes narrowed as she watched me. "Why not?"

"Because it's this," I replied.

I handed her the key fob and slid out of the vehicle. I turned to face her through the open door. "I need you to trust me and not come after me no matter what happens. You'll stay right here. Promise me that."

"Finn, I don't think—"

I cut her off. "Dara, this is important. Please promise me."

She hesitated, then nodded. "I promise."

"Good," I said with what I hoped was a confident smile. "I think this vehicle is bulletproof, which is why the Don chose it for us. Stay in here and keep the doors locked. I'll be back as soon as I can." I shoved the door shut and walked away.

Chapter Eight

I HEARD DARA SAY my name as I made my way across the huge parking lot, but I didn't stop until I reached the front of the mall. I felt small, standing there looking at the metal plates that covered the top to bottom windows we had broken. Even the second story windows were plated. There was no way I could get inside by myself. Fortunately, I had another stupid plan. Vicken would be proud.

I put my hands to my mouth and gave a long, low howl.

A tense minute later, the sound of footsteps reached my ears. I stepped back until I was standing on the sidewalk in front of the parking lot. I watched as guards in full gear jogged from either side of the mall. Their guns were ready, but they kept in ranks as their followed their leaders to the center. When there were at least three dozen of them in staggered formation, the procession halted. Thirty-six guns pointed in my direction. My heart slowed.

The leader in gray who stood near the left side of the guards pushed her goggles up and pulled off her helmet.

Madam Opal gave me a humorless smile. "I told them you'd be back." She shot one of the other leaders a look. "They wanted to hunt you down and make you pay for freeing one of our highly valuable displays, but I told them you were more valuable and you would come back of your own accord."

"You have something I want," I replied.

"Your baby sister," she guessed.

I nodded. "I'm not leaving without her."

"That's true," she replied. "Because you're not leaving."

She drew her gun and fired from the hip. The bullet slammed into my chest hard enough to crack ribs. I fell to the pavement. My teeth clenched so hard I felt the side of my tongue start to bleed where it had been caught between them. The shock of electricity hurt even worse than I remembered. Madam Opal's face blocked out the blinding light of the rising sun. I closed my eyes and fought to remain conscious.

"Carry him to the main display. I'll be along shortly to show him how we deal with traitors," she said.

The sound of the metal plates sliding up was harsh to my overly sensitive ears. Even though the electricity had stopped, I felt as though every nerve ending was frayed. When the guards picked me up, the places their hands held felt as though they were scorched. I had to will myself to remain silent so they would think I was unconscious.

They walked up the steps without bothering to be gentle. Keeping my eyes open just a crack, I watched the doors pass by followed by the sweeping ceiling of the entrance corridor.

I heard the bang as the plates in front of the doors slid shut once more. It sounded as though it sealed my doom.

My instincts beckoned for me to fight before I was thrown into one of the barred cages and it became too late. But I bided my time and forced myself to concentrate on my toes. It was a strange exercise, something I had never done before, and with the adrenaline pounding beneath my skin and my limbs still held in paralysis, it felt like a vain task. But I didn't give up. With each step the guards took, I found that my toes responded a little bit more. As soon as I could move them completely, I shifted my focus to my fingers. I kept my lidded gaze on the ceiling. I didn't have enough time. I had to make it count.

We were almost to the escalator, I was sure of it. One more step, just one more. Their footfalls hit the tiled floor like the tromp of a herd of elephants. As soon as the last one fell, I channeled my strength and pushed off.

Surprised, the guards let me drop. The instant my feet touched the floor, I took off running toward the caged rooms on the far side of the escalator. My legs responded sluggishly and I ended up in a half-skip run; it wasn't pretty, but it would have to do.

"Stop him!" someone shouted.

I watched Vicken turn from his seat on his bed and saw his eyes widen when he spotted me with what was probably the entire horde of guards chasing me down. I lowered my shoulder, pushed forward even faster, and felt at least six bullets hit my back and legs at the same time.

Fortunately, their impact actually helped the momentum of my haphazard run. As the paralysis took over, I slammed into the bars hard enough that it threatened to jar my teeth from my skull. I slumped to the ground with Vicken's face hovering above me.

"Finn, why did you come back?" he demanded, his voice tight with worry.

With my jaw locked, I couldn't have said anything. But one glance as the hands of the guards hauled me back showed that I had done what I intended. Vicken followed my gaze to where the bars met the floor. The force of my impact had broken several of them free. Vicken's eyes widened and he hurried quickly to the other end of the cage to take the guards' attention away.

"He tried to kill me!" he shouted. "Get that feral werewolf away from me! He's dangerous!"

I wanted to roll my eyes at his theatrics, but at that moment, my heart was wondering if receiving so many bullets had been a good idea.

A loud humming sound filled my ears along with the slower-than-usual thumping of my heart.

"How many of you shot him?" Madam Opal demanded in a shrill voice.

She could have stood above me or been in the next room for all my senses said. Everything spun, and with my eyes closed, I had no way to make it stop.

"Take him to Sir Harbrand!" she ordered. "Tell him I want this werewolf fit for display by this afternoon."

"Yes, Madam Opal," a man replied.

Hands grabbed me and the present faded to a fuzzy blur. Footsteps ran together, doors beeped, rooms echoed, and the rushing sound continued. I lost track of how long I wandered in my mind. It was nice and relaxing; no need drove me and no thought stayed solid for longer than a second. I enjoyed it until something struck my chest so hard I fought for breath.

"That's it," a familiar voice said. "Breathe or die. That's the way of things. Normally I'm fine if you choose either option, but Madam Opal was very clear about what would happen if I let you die on my table."

My body felt hot and cold at the same time. Tremors ran over my skin while my heart beat angrily in my chest. I was relieved when my eyes opened at my command. I squinted.

"Sorry. It's a bit bright." The lights dimmed and I found myself looking up at Sir Harbrand. "I'd say no hard feelings, but that would be a lie." He glared at me. "You caused mass hysteria with my students. They'll always fear werewolves now."

"Good," I said between gritted teeth.

A light of humor shone in Sir Harbrand's eyes. "So the werewolf has a bit of fire, does he? Maybe Madam Opal was right. It's better that animals stay animals."

"What does that mean?" I asked. I tried to lift my hand, but it didn't move. I glanced down and saw that my limbs were attached to the table. Sir Harbrand hadn't used the leather straps that contained Donessa Ruvine, either; this time, he had wrapped full chains along each arm and leg. "What's going on?" I demanded.

Sir Harbrand gave a small smile. "A bit much, don't you think? So did I before they showed me the damage you did when you broke the other monsters out of here. Now, I'm not leaving anything to chance." His smile turned sickly. "Not if I want to keep my head. There's a few waiting to be cremated down stairs thanks to your last endeavors and I'll be trying my hardest not to join them, thank you very much."

The man looked a bit more frazzled than the last time I had seen him. His black hair wasn't quite as slicked back and strands had worked free to tangle in front of his red bandana. Sir Harbrand's mustache was no longer curled at the ends, and his short-trimmed beard contained pieces of something I couldn't identify.

He nodded toward the other end of the room. "Edgart, bring the stone."

I strained my eyes to follow Sir Harbrand's assistant. The young man skirted around the table as far as he could go before he reached Sir Harbrand. By the way he refused to meet my gaze, I knew I had indeed left an impression. I allowed a grim smile to touch my lips.

"Smiling, are we?" Sir Harbrand said. "Better enjoy it. It'll be the last smile you have for a long time." He winked at his assistant. "It's a bit hard to smile as a wolf."

Edgart gave a nervous chuckle.

"What are you talking about?" I asked.

Sir Harbrand indicated the tray Edgart held. "What do you know about moonstones, my boy?"

The word brought back something Lark had said when we first took her to the Academy. "I knew of a Remus," she had said. "He was also a werewolf, but they used a moonstone to keep him in wolf form to see if staying an animal would eventually make him think like one. It was pretty cruel if you ask me. I could tell he missed being in his human form."

A whisper of panic started at the back of my mind. "Don't bring that near me," I said. I strained against the chains.

"What? Afraid of your animal side?" Sir Harbrand asked with a hint of glee in his tone.

I held his gaze. "You should be afraid of my animal side," I growled.

The man merely shook his head. "Unfortunately for you, Madam Opal is the one who commanded me to implant you with the moonstone. Her angry side has far more bite than I suspect yours does."

I didn't know how I would ever have a chance to rescue Amelia or Vicken if I was trapped in wolf form. I struggled against the chains, but Sir Harbrand hadn't taken any chances.

"Let me go!" I yelled.

"Sorry," Sir Harbrand replied without the least bit of apology in his tone. "This is going to hurt a bit."

He held out a hand to Edgart. The young man placed a scalpel on his palm.

Sweat broke out across my skin when Sir Harbrand put a gloved hand on my bare chest. He touched the scalpel to a spot just below my right collarbone and pressed down. A yell tore from my lips when he cut deeper, opening the wound wide.

"The moonstone," he said.

Edgart set a small brown rock in Sir Harbrand's hand. The man met my gaze. "Needless to say, while we call this a moonstone, it is actually a piece of a meteorite from the moon." He held it up. "It's hard to believe that this little rock used to be up in space."

"What brought it here?" Edgart asked.

Sir Harbrand glanced at him. "It was ejected from the moon by the impact of an asteroidal meteoroid or maybe a comet. It rarely happens, so when they land here on earth, they're worth a pretty penny." He winked at me. "Madam Opal has quite the corner on the black market for such things."

The feeling of my warm blood flowing down my shoulder wasn't a pleasant one. I struggled against the chains again, but it was no use. Even being this close to the moonstone made my muscles ache with the need to phase.

"This'll take just a minute," Sir Harbrand said. "Have patience."

The moment the moonstone touched my skin, I couldn't fight the phase.

"He's changing!" Edgart said with fear in his voice.

"Grab the muzzle," Sir Harbrand instructed as he worked quickly at my shoulder. I felt the bite of the staples he used to close the wound even as my shoulders rolled and form changed.

"Get ready," Sir Harbrand commanded.

"I'm ready," Edgart replied, his voice shaky.

My arms slid free of the chains as they phased into the more slender limbs of a wolf. As soon as my legs had changed as well, I spun and lunged off the table. Unfortunately, Sir Harbrand was ready. An electric bullet impacted my side and I fell heavily to the floor.

Edgart slipped the muzzle over my face before I could regain the strength to attack. By the time I had any control over my body, both Sir Harbrand and Edgart were standing over me admiring their work.

"How long will that keep him a wolf?" Edgart asked.

"As long as it's in his body," Sir Harbrand replied with a satisfied expression.

I lifted my lips in a weak snarl. Neither of them appeared the least bit afraid of my paralyzed ferocity.

"Let's get him to a cage before he comes around completely." Sir Harbrand said.

To my dismay, the two of them sunk their hands into my fur and dragged me toward the door.

"He's heavy!" Edgart protested.

"His mass doesn't change from man to wolf, it merely shifts form, so he weighs as much as a wolf." He grimaced as he dragged me to a cart. "But it does make for a massive animal."

I lay there helplessly as they drove out of the infirmary and around the escalators to the far end of the training grounds. To my chagrin, Sir Harbrand then pressed the button on an elevator hidden behind a fake building in the corner. That would have made our escape earlier much easier.

When the elevator beeped and the door opened, Sir Harbrand drove us along the second floor to a display cage near the Maes' meeting room. I wondered where the feathered woman I had seen in there before had gone, but I couldn't ask.

Edgart unlocked the door and I was pulled unceremoniously inside. He unbuckled the muzzle and backed quickly away, slamming the door behind him even though I couldn't move.

"Double check that lock," Sir Harbrand commanded. "Madam Opal will have our heads if he escapes, and I mean that literally."

Edgart checked the door one more time, then backed away. "He is secure, Sir."

Sir Harbrand nodded. I wished I could turn away from his interested gaze, but the electric bullet still had me in its paralyzing hold.

"Good, good," he said. He rubbed his hands together like a child about to receive a much-anticipated gift. "Let the training begin."

He drove away and left me to ponder what that meant. But thinking was hard. With the moonstone below my collarbone, the effects were hard to ignore. My thoughts became disjointed, need-driven, pack-oriented, and filled with sounds, smells, and images instead of words. I thought of the girl sitting in the SUV waiting for me. Panic gripped my mind at the realization that I couldn't remember her name. Instead, her smell, the way her footsteps sounded, and the rising of my heart whenever she was near surfaced at the thought of her. My human side was already slipping away.

As soon as I could move, I pushed to my feet. My head hung low, heavy with exhaustion from the paralysis. But my need to find my baby sister pressed against me. I had never seen her or smelled her, yet the whisper of pack and the need to protect her drove me to check every edge of the cage. My strength slowly returned as I paced, but I couldn't find a weakness in either the bars or the walls. This enclosure no longer even contained a bed. The walls were bare and the floor covered by only a threadbare carpet. When I scratched at it, I found cement beneath.

The need to escape kept me pacing throughout the day. Members of the Society pointed as they walked by, and I could hear them speaking of the wolf behind the bars, but after only a few hours, their words no longer made sense. Panic pressed against me and made me pace again, but I didn't know if I was running toward something or away. Only the thought that two members of my pack were in trouble kept me centered.

I remembered Vicken. Though his name was elusive, thoughts of the pale-skinned, fanged vampire surfaced over and over again in my mind. I hung onto the memory of him behind the bars, calling to me when we drove away. Much of the memory didn't make sense any longer, but the look in his eyes stayed with me. There was pleading and despair in them, yes, but also trust. He trusted that I would come back for him. He was part of my pack, and he needed my help. The heart of a wolf was loyal above all else.

Toward the end of the day, the door to the meeting room opened again and my teeth bared of their own accord.

A woman with white hair pulled back in a bun advanced to the cage. As she walked toward me, an expression of adoration warred with contempt on her face. She said something to the man next to her, and though the words didn't mean anything to me, their tone made my ears lay back against my skull. When they stopped a few feet from the cage, my silent snarl rose to a deafening growl.

"…manners…," my brain understood out of the string of words she said.

At the woman's gesture, the man pulled a stick out of his belt. He pressed a button and blue light sparked between the prongs at the end. I snarled at them and made the mistake of sticking my muzzle out between the bars. The man touched the stick to it. The ensuing shock sent me back with a yelp. I growled louder and launched myself at the bars in an effort to reach him and tear him apart. He shocked me again and again. Each time I fell back, I jumped at the bars again. I wouldn't show them any cowardice or weakness. They might have caged my body, but my mind wasn't weak and my heart refused to give up.

The woman laughed and goaded him into shocking me over and over. While the voice in the back of my mind reasoned that I should hang back and reserve my strength, the wolf side of me was mindless with fury at being trapped and tormented. With the hold of the moon streaming through the windows overhead and the control of the moonstone in my shoulder, my wolf side took precedence. I didn't care how often I hit the bars hard enough to jar my mind; I ignored the way the sparks from the stick made answering flashes appear behind my eyes. I would fight him as long as he stood there. I would prove to her that I was a danger. I would fight until I no longer had the strength to do so.

Eventually, I collapsed against the bars. The man stuck me again with the stick, but though it hurt, I no longer had the strength to move. A weak yelp escaped me at the second-to-last prod, then I had nothing left. At the woman's word, the man stopped. She said something else and they both turned to walk away. I listened to their footsteps disappear, then allowed my mind to go black.

When I opened my eyes, the woman was back. The windows on the roof showed that a new day had dawned. I felt anxious about that, but couldn't say why. Next to the woman stood a small girl. She held something in her hand. I willed my eyes to focus on it as I stood. It was a weapon. Pain would come from it, that much was sure. It seemed the appearance of the woman was destined to cause pain. I hated her even though I couldn't put into words why.

With the sunlight overhead instead of the moon, I was better able to contain my instincts. I didn't attack the bars, I merely sat behind them and watched the pair with the knowledge that I couldn't escape what was coming. Or could I? A thought struck me, an impulse hinted at through desperation. Wolves didn't do well behind bars. The wolf side of me was ready to give whatever rational thoughts I could muster a chance in the name of survival. It was worth a shot.

Given the weapon in her hand, the young girl was my biggest threat. I wanted to direct my anger toward the woman with the white hair, but something told me she gave the orders for others to act upon. If I could stop the action, maybe I could slow her torture for a bit.

I found a memory that I felt would work and focused on the girl. I could hear Professor Mellon's voice in my mind. Some of the words made sense. I forced my mind to focus on them and put them together.

"Let down your walls. Pull inward like you're taking a breath through your fingertips."

I did the opposite. Instead of pulling in, I pushed toward the little girl using my muzzle instead of my fingertips as a focal point. I wasn't sure it would work given my form and the distance between us, but then the girl's gaze widened. I shut my eyes and let the memory flow.

At four years old, I sat on my mother's bed. Drake, only three at the time, played with blocks on the floor. Something was wrong with my mom. Dad had said she was sick and that we should give her space, but she didn't want space. She wanted us there with her for as long as we possibly could be. I played with my action figures near her pillow. She smiled as I reenacted a ferocious battle. The fighting was intense;

plastic swords clashed and I made the most of the sounds my dad had taught me when we played together.

"Mine."

Drake grabbed one of the toy soldiers.

"No, mine," I replied, taking it back.

Drake started to cry. I stared from him to Mom. Dad had said that if we did anything to upset her, we had to leave the room.

"I'm sorry, Drakey," I quickly apologized. I handed him back the toy. "You can have it."

"No!" Drake replied. He threw the soldier against the wall and cried even harder.

I looked back at Mom. "I'm sorry. I'll make it better."

I slipped off the bed and knelt in front of Drake.

"Please calm down. I'm sorry. You can play with my toys anytime, I promise. Just stop crying," I pleaded.

I looked down the hall, certain Dad would show up at any moment and usher us out, but the door remained empty.

"Drakey, you need to calm down, you know why?"

Drake slowed his crying at my question. He shook his head, his eyes still filled with tears.

I brushed a tear off his cheek with my fingers. "Because Mommy is sick. We can't be loud if Mommy is sick. She needs us to be quiet and happy so we can help her feel better. You want her to feel better, don't you?"

Drake nodded and sniffed. "Yes," he said.

I nodded. "That's because you're a big boy and you understand. You know we need to be quiet and happy for Mommy."

Drake nodded again. "I'll be quiet."

I picked up the soldier and handed it to him. He took it with a grin and started playing the way I had been.

I looked up and saw tears in Mom's eyes. I hurried quickly back to her side.

"I'm sorry, Mommy. I didn't mean to make him upset. He's okay now. Are you?"

My mother pushed my unruly hair back from my face and smiled at me through her tears. "Yes, Finn, I'm okay. I don't want you to worry. Everything is going to be okay."

That was the last time my mother spoke to me before she passed away. When I opened my eyes to the present, tears rolled down my muzzle and dropped to the floor.

"Wolves don't cry," Madam Opal said. "What's wrong with him?"

The fact that I understood her didn't lessen the sorrow that lingered from the memory. I wondered if remembering being human had helped my brain grasp using language again.

"Shoot him," she commanded.

A glance at the young girl showed the same tears in her eyes. She lifted the gun, her hand shaking, only to lower it again and shake her head.

"What is wrong with you?" Madam Opal demanded.

I snarled and they both backed up. Madam Opal ripped the gun from the young girl's hand and shot it at me. Instead of the electric bullet, probes pierced my skin. The electricity that surged through me dropped me to the floor. The last thing I saw was Madam Opal's face twisted in anger before I blacked out.

Chapter Nine

"MAYBE THE MOONSTONE IS too much for him." Sir Harbrand's voice penetrated the darkness.

"Maybe werewolves are weaker than we thought. He's an Alpha. He should be stronger than this," Madam Opal replied.

"He was shot by half a dozen bullets. That would have killed a human right off. As it was, I had to use adrenaline to revive him again. I don't recommend using any more electricity. His heart won't take much more," Sir Harbrand recommended.

"Pathetic," Madam Opal sneered. "A werewolf that can't take a bullet. How disappointing."

Sir Harbrand's voice was hopeful when he said, "Maybe we should terminate him now so we can perform an autopsy. We'd probably learn more."

"He's the only werewolf we have until that whelp grows up," Madam Opal said. "Let's not be hasty. How is the infant doing, anyway?"

"Not well." Sir Harbrand's voice didn't contain any empathy when he said, "It refuses a bottle and cries nonstop. I've a mind to perform an autopsy on it, instead."

"If you do, your head will be the one having an autopsy," Madam Opal warned. "Get the whelp to eat, or else."

Her words hung in the air as her footsteps faded away. I realized by the smell of antiseptic and pain that I was back in the infirmary. I opened my eyes to find that I was still in wolf form, but bound to the table.

"My head will be the one having the autopsy indeed," Sir Harbrand muttered. "Who will be the one doing it if I'm not around?"

He stood at the other end of the room with his back to me. Edgart was nowhere to be seen. I flexed my muscles to test the bonds. Either Sir Harbrand hadn't thought me a threat in my weakened state, or Madam Opal had harried him to work quickly. Either way, the straps that held me to the table were leather instead of chain, and no muzzle prevented me from using my fangs. If I could reach my head back far enough, I could chew my way through.

Reasoning as a wolf wasn't the easiest thing. My instincts demanded that I get out of the weak position, but it was only through sheer concentration that I could think of how to make that happen. If I broke the bonds with Sir Harbrand ready to react, he could shoot me before I got free completely. My best option was to create a state of terror. From what I had seen, he didn't do well under panic.

He was worried about my heart. By the sound of the monitor near my head, they were monitoring my heartbeat in case of irregularity. Just thinking of my heart made it give a small flutter. There was no doubt in my mind that it had been damaged by the electricity. The question was if I could use that to my advantage without killing myself in the process. I had heard of people who could make their heartbeat slow down by concentrating. I wondered if I could do the same.

It was a messed-up plan and I felt a brief longing for Vicken to be near so I could tell it to him. His dismay always goaded me into action. As it was, he was locked behind bars and I was strapped to a table; neither of us seemed to be getting very far.

I concentrated on my heartbeat until it thundered in my ears. Then, very carefully, I thought of it skipping a beat. Just like earlier with the flutter, my heart gave a little skip. It scared me and thrilled me at the same time. Maybe my plan wasn't so idiotic as it sounded.

When I concentrated, it skipped again. I felt my lungs catch strangely in my chest and my forearms went numb for a moment. The thought that I was doing further damage remained forefront in my mind. The question was how much I could take and still free Vicken and Amelia.

This time when I did it, it caught Sir Harbrand's attention. He hurried to the table and studied the monitor while I pretended to still be unconscious. He turned away and I made my heart skip again.

"That's not good," Sir Harbrand muttered.

He leaned over the table to check my pulse. The second his fingers touched my neck, I turned and latched onto his hand.

Sir Harbrand yelped in pain. "Let go, let go, let go!" he pleaded. "I need my fingers!"

I gave a low growl and bit down harder.

"Alright, alright!" he cried. "What do you want? Freedom? Of course you want freedom. Hold on. Let me call for—"

I growled again and felt his bones grind beneath my fangs.

"Wait!" he shrieked. "Wait! Don't do that!"

He fumbled with his free hand for the strap across my shoulders. As soon as it was free, I slipped from under the other set, still careful to keep his hand secure.

"You're free," Sir Harbrand stammered. "Wha-what now?"

I looked from him to the door.

"Uh, right," he said. "You can't open doors. Let me help you."

I jumped down from the table careful to keep the same pressure on his hand. He cried out in pain just the same. The thought occurred to me that I should have him remove the moonstone while he was at it, but the reality was that the stress of phasing back to human form might put my heart over the edge for good. I had to give it a chance to heal before exerting it again.

Sir Harbrand opened the door. When I didn't release him, he followed me docilely toward the exit. I hesitated at the door to the training grounds. I knew what kind of ammunition the guards inside were packing. If Sir Harbrand yelled at all, I wouldn't have a chance to track down the others. But it was the only way out that I knew of.

When I growled, Sir Harbrand pushed the door open. We were almost to the escalator, his keycard out and my muscles bunched as I readied myself to dash up the stairs, when a guard appeared.

"What's going on?" he asked.

The man's eyes went from Sir Harbrand to me, then to Sir Harbrand's hand in my mouth. The blood must have answered his question even if Sir Harbrand was too afraid to speak.

"Escapee!" he yelled.

I let my instincts take over completely.

As swiftly as a wolf takes down a deer, I darted at Sir Harbrand's legs and bit down on the back of his ankle. I felt his Achilles tendon snap; he let out a howl of pain and crumpled to the floor clutching his leg. The guard had his gun out and was aiming it, but I sprang before he could pull the trigger. My jaws clamped around his hand as he shouted for help.

The sound of running footsteps met my ears. Knowing I had probably sealed my fate, I took off for the back of the training grounds. One guard spotted me, then another. They followed me with shouts and calls for backup.

I lost track of how many twists and turns I took around the grounds. At several points, I ran across monsters chained to their posts. I wanted to free them, but at that moment, my life was the one in danger. I couldn't get up the escalator without a keycard, and I had no way to use one if I found it. I had trapped myself as effectively as if I was back in the cage on display, but now there were hostile guards on my tail and no one to call them off. How was I supposed to save Vicken and Amelia if I couldn't even get myself out of trouble?

I raced around a stand of cutout trees, darted past three guards, then cut a corner and ran back the way I had come, which put me past seven others. My goal was to hide somewhere in the city in the hopes that I could catch my breath and figure out a plan. But the second I left the forest area, my exhausted heart skipped a beat and my paws followed. I tripped and rolled, landing hard against the corner of a building.

My breath wheezed in my throat as I struggled to my feet. The footsteps weren't far behind.

"He's over there!" someone shouted.

Shots struck the wood next to my head. I ducked between the fake buildings and ran as though my life depended on it, because it did. Unfortunately, my life also appeared to depend on not running.

Just as the thought crossed my mind, my heart skipped another beat. This time I tumbled into a wall. I fought to get up, but my legs were numb and didn't want to respond. When I finally pushed up to my paws, I found myself looking into the faces of a dozen guards.

"Hold still, freak," the closest one said.

A bullet hit me in the chest. He laughed.

"My turn," another called out.

A bullet hit me in the right forearm. It crumpled beneath me and I fell twitching to the floor.

"Now it's my turn," the next said.

He stepped forward and put his gun against my skull. I could only look at him, angry, paralyzed, in pain, and with no way to fight back. At that range, it would kill me.

"You're overdue," he said. His finger tightened on the trigger.

I closed my eyes. A shout sounded, then another. The pressure of the gun muzzle let up, but the bullet didn't fire. It didn't make sense. I opened my eyes and could only stare.

Carnage was everywhere. The guards had been torn apart as though some massive predator had gotten ahold of them. I wondered through the pain in my chest who the predator could be. I braced myself for a monster who would tear me apart like the humans. When he appeared again behind one of the city buildings, I fell back in relief to the floor.

Vicken shook his head. "I know. It took me long enough. I had to wait for night and the bars weren't nearly as loose as they looked. It took some time to…are you alright?"

I sucked in a breath through my nose and let it out through my mouth. My heart was pounding strangely. For the moment, it felt as though Sir Harbrand had given me one of his adrenaline injections. I pushed to my feet.

"Alright," Vicken said. "You need to phase so we can get out of here. There's no way I can hide you like that."

I snorted.

Vicken's eyebrows pulled together. "Seriously? You want to stay like that?"

I gave a huff of frustration at the fact that we were getting nowhere and we were running out of time very quickly.

"Fine," Vicken said. "Have it your way, but let's hurry."

He ran to the escalator. I followed closely at his heels with the worry that whatever fueled my strength would quickly be giving out.

At least Vicken had a keycard. He opened the door to the escalator and we ran up. Scents touched my nose and I growled before we reached the top.

"What is it?" Vicken asked. "Guards?"

I nodded.

"Right." His eyes narrowed as he talked. He looked around. "At least the escalator isn't moving. Must be a lockdown protocol or something. It'll give us the element of surprise." He pulled out the guns he had taken from the fallen guards below. "Let's do this."

I darted up the stairs in front of him before he could react. I figured that if I could catch their attention, he would have the element of surprise. When I leaped up the last five steps and landed at the top, I found myself in a stare down between at least ten guards and myself. With the amount of guns pointed in my direction, it was a losing battle.

"Freeze," one of the guards yelled.

I took off to the right as fast as my paws would carry me. My claws scrabbled across the cement as bullets whizzed by my head. My plan was to circle around them and come up from behind to deal with those Vicken missed, but by the time the guards realized they were being fired upon, he had taken down half of them. When I circled back, the rest were lying in a heap on the ground.

"Smart thinking," the vampire said when I reached him.

My head hung low and I struggled to pull in a breath.

"What's wrong?" he asked. "Did you get shot?"

Vicken dropped to his knees and ran his hands quickly over me. When he backed up, the symptoms refused to go away.

"I don't understand," he said. "You weren't shot."

I gritted my teeth and tried to force my head up, but my feet gave out. I fell heavily to the floor.

"Finn!" Vicken shouted. He shook me. "Finn, what's going on?"

I tried to respond, but my heart chose at that moment to skip another beat. My breath caught in my throat and I winced at the pain.

"Finn, this isn't the time to be fooling around. We've got to find your little sister," Vicken lectured as if I wasn't taking things seriously.

Something caught in my throat and I coughed. With each cough, my heart skipped a beat. By the time I was done, pinkish-white foam covered my muzzle. I looked up at Vicken.

"That's blood," he said, his voice soft. "Finn, you're in serious trouble."

Without saying another word, he picked me up with an ease I envied and slung me across his shoulders like a wolf skin mantle. When he turned and ran through the parking garage instead of up the next escalator, I thought he was insane. He slowed next to a huge truck at the far end and pulled open the door. Placing me on the seat, he tore out the cover beneath the steering wheel and yanked down some wires. He stripped two with his teeth, then twisted them together. The truck rumbled to life.

He slid up into the driver's seat and shifted the truck into drive. When he glanced at me, his cheeks held the barest brush of color. "What?" he asked. "So I was a troubled youth."

I had never heard of a troubled vampire, but I had also never heard of a vampire youth who hotwired cars. Either way, we were outside of my knowledge base. And to top it off, the coughing picked up again.

"Hold on," Vicken said. He put a hand on my side. "Tell your heart to keep pumping. Don't give up."

I wanted to tell him to hurry, but couldn't have said anything even if I wasn't in wolf form. A groan escaped me at the pain in my chest. Vicken's jaw jutted forward in determination.

"I'm getting us out of here."

He steered the truck around the parking lot. I couldn't look out the window to see where we were going, but he didn't slow down. He glanced at me once and said, "Hang on." He realized I had no ability to hang onto anything and grabbed the fur of my neck in his steel grip before he pressed the pedal down to the floor.

"If the gate is stronger than this truck, we're in trouble," he muttered. "It's our only shot."

He glanced at me, then leaned forward with his shoulders hunched and eyes intent on whatever he saw outside the windshield. I heard several yells, saw the skin around Vicken's eyes tighten, then a crash shook the truck. His eyes widened again and he drove forward.

He glanced at me. "The gate was weaker."

My eyes closed against my will.

"No, don't do that," Vicken said. He shook me by my ruff. "Stay with me."

He looked out the window. "Is that Dara?"

The truck slowed, then stopped. He got out and I heard arguing voices.

"Where's Finn?" Dara demanded.

"In the truck. Something's wrong with him. He needs help right away," Vicken replied.

"What's wrong with him?"

"I don't know what's wrong with him!"

"Was he shot?" Dara asked, her voice tight.

Vicken replied, "No, he wasn't shot, I don't think. But he's coughing up bloody foam. I think his heart's failing."

"What! What do you mean, his heart's failing?"

"The foam," Vicken said. "It's a sign. He's, well, look at him."

He pulled open the door behind me. Dara set a hand on my back. I felt her pull, but couldn't do anything to stop her. Her hand slid away.

"Dara? Dara!" Silence, then, "I've got you. Take it easy. Are you alright?"

"It's his heart; you're right," I heard her reply, her voice weak. "But I don't know what happened. He can't show me. He's in some sort of daze."

"We have to get him to help," Vicken said.

"But where? Who knows what to do for a werewolf?"

"Other werewolves."

Through the haze that filled my mind, I heard Dara's confused reply, followed by Vicken saying, "Grayson apparently found a werewolf pack in the city. They're not far from here."

"You're going to ask them for help?"

"Who else?" Vicken asked. "There is no one else. Vampires won't know what to do and the Academy is too far away. He'd never make it. He needs help now, and we've got to get out of here before anyone realizes we're gone."

"Fine, but I'm going with you," Dara insisted.

"I wouldn't have it any other way," Vicken replied. I heard him run around to the driver's side of the truck.

Dara slipped behind my seat into the back. I was glad she chose not to touch me again. I had no idea if my damaged heart could hurt hers, but I didn't want to take a chance.

When Vicken climbed in and started the truck, Dara asked, "Why wouldn't you have it any other way?"

Vicken replied, "Because you're the sweeter of the two of us. They might listen to you."

"Great," Dara said from behind me. "If I'm the sweet one, we're all in trouble."

Vicken muttered as he drove. Sometimes the words made sense to me, other times, my mind drifted off. I had another coughing fit and then struggled to breathe afterwards. Dara didn't touch me, but kept whispering to me encouragingly, telling me to hang on and that I had to pull through. She wanted me to promise her that I wouldn't give up, but even my eyes wouldn't open so I could promise her with a look. If there was anything I could do to not leave her side, I would do it. I hoped thinking the promise was enough.

"This is it."

"Looks a bit scary," Dara commented.

Vicken slid to a stop and I heard him run around the truck. He certainly did a lot of running even though he took pleasure in chiding me for the same thing. I figured I should point that out when I was able to.

The door opened, and then I was being carried up a long set of stairs. Vicken banged on a door. The sound echoed strangely inside.

"Nobody's answering," Dara said, her voice tight with anxiety. "Why isn't anybody answering?"

"Maybe they didn't hear," Vicken replied. He banged on the door again loud enough to be heard two states away. Still nobody answered.

Vicken backed down several stairs and then looked up and called out, "Hey, I have one of your werewolves. He's dying! He needs help!"

My heart gave a beat so hard I winced. It beat again and I groaned with the pain.

"Did you hear me?" Vicken shouted with panic in his voice. "He's dying! Can't you see that? You need to help him!"

Another coughing fit hit me. Vicken knelt on the steps and set me down gently.

"Come on, buddy. Breathe. Just breathe and keep that heart beating. Don't you give up now."

I tried to suck in a breath, but I couldn't. My chest hurt, my head hurt, and the world spun when I opened my eyes. I tried to stretch to open my lungs, but only pain followed. I felt myself slipping away.

"No, Finn, don't do that," Dara said. She reached for me.

"Don't touch him," Vicken warned.

Dara's fingers brushed my shoulder. I felt her pull. My eyes flew open. I tried to stop her. My heart would kill her. I didn't want to be the death of the girl I loved. My heart gave another hard beat and we both winced. I closed my eyes and felt her fall to my side. The sound of a door opening behind me was the last thing I heard.

Chapter Ten

"STAY OUTSIDE."

"But we're his friends!" Vicken's voice with filled with exasperation and fear.

"Werewolves aren't friends with vampires and whatever she is."

"She's an empath."

"Then she should know how much I hate you both."

"She would if she were awake, but she fainted when she touched him!" The panic in the vampire's voice beat against me, but I couldn't open my eyes to see what was going on.

"An empath should know better than to touch someone with heart failure."

"She loves him."

Silence followed. The sound of their argument still bounced around painfully in my skull. I put my ears back, but it didn't help.

"He's probably dead."

"Can you at least try?" Vicken pleaded. "I can't lose them. They…they rescued me from the Maes."

"Why on earth would a werewolf and an empath rescue a vampire? It doesn't make any sense," the gruff voice asked.

"Because we're friends," Vicken replied. I know I didn't imagine the strain in his voice when he said, "Best friends. You've got to save them."

Another moment of silence followed.

Finally, the gruff voice said, "Follow me."

"I-I can't carry them both." The desperation in Vicken's voice made it sound like he was close to tears.

"Give me the werewolf. You carry the girl."

The sound of a massive door shutting was followed by footsteps that echoed as if in an empty hallway.

After a few seconds of walking, Vicken said, "You really should hire a decorator."

"And you should shut your trap before I shut it for you," the man who carried me growled.

I could almost feel how badly Vicken wanted to reply. It wasn't like the vampire to keep quiet after a comment like that. It made me want to see the frustration on his face. I tried to force my eyes open. They obeyed just long enough for me to glimpse a black and gray marble floor, a pair of worn work boots, and Vicken's black leather shoes that appeared to be in far worse condition than he ever allowed them to be at Haunted High. My eyes closed again of their own accord and my head spun at the effort.

"Here."

"In here?" The disgust in Vicken's voice was nearly palpable.

"Yes, in here," the man snapped. "What? Do you think I have some sort of hospital wing I'm hiding away? That I always allow wretched kids in here to criticize my home? Do you want to leave?"

His last question hung in the air.

Vicken's voice was somber when he said, "I'm sorry. I appreciate you letting us in here. Please don't make us leave."

It was the most apologetic I had ever heard the vampire. He must be truly worried. My heart gave a painful thump at the thought that I was the one causing his problems. The heartbeat sent a surge of pain through my chest and my body spasmed. I tried to curl inward in an attempt to stop the pain.

"What's happening?" Vicken asked worriedly.

"It's his heart," the man replied. "It's not beating evenly."

"How do you know that?"

"I can hear it," he answered gruffly. "It's a werewolf thing."

"So you are a werewolf!" the triumph in the vampire's voice was edged with fear.

"Isn't that why you brought him here?" the man asked drily.

"Yes, but I wasn't sure I could find you."

The man set me on a cold, hard surface.

"Where can I put Dara?"

"Over there," the man directed. "Her pulse sounds steady. I don't think she's in the danger he is. Right now, she needs to sleep and I need your help with him."

I heard items be shoved off a surface, and then Vicken's familiar footsteps walked to the table.

"Is he, uh…." Vicken's question faded away.

"Going to die?" the man replied gruffly. "I don't know. His heart isn't beating nearly enough to supply his brain. There could be damage if we don't move quickly enough. What happened to him?"

"I-I don't know," Vicken replied. "He was caged by the Maes and they use these electric probes for training, but he was shot before, and he ran into my cage hard enough to loosen the bars so I could get out, but it took me so long because I had to wait until the coast was clear, and when I found him, he was surrounded by guards. Some of them had already shot him, and one had a gun to his head—"

"Alright, alright," the man barked. "Shut up!"

I had never heard Vicken run on like that in my life. The fear that filled his voice made his words stammer. My heart clenched at the pain in his tone and the thought that I had caused it. My body started to shake. I couldn't control it.

"What's happening to him?" Vicken asked.

"I don't know," the man replied. "Get me that over there."

"This?"

"No, that!"

My body shook so hard my teeth were rattling. I couldn't draw in a full breath. I felt like I was suffocating.

Something pierced my skin. A yelp of pain escaped me, and then warmth flooded my body. The shaking slowed and then stopped. I was able to draw in a full breath. My muscles eased and my head settled back on the table.

"What was that?" Vicken asked.

"A sedative. His body is in shock. It could kill him with his heart the way it is."

"But won't a sedative affect his heart, too?" Vicken's voice was tight when he asked, "Did you just kill him?"

"No," the man replied, followed by an uncertain, "I hope not. For now, at least, his heartbeat is steady. It's slower than it should be, but he's alive. Our goal is to keep him that way until nightfall."

My thoughts were getting fuzzy and sluggish. It was harder to follow their conversation.

"What happens at night?"

"The moon," the man said in a tone that didn't hide the fact that he thought Vicken was slow. I forced my mind to focus though the haze that filled it so I could hear him say, "Werewolves need the moon. I can amplify the effects with my mirrors and crystals, but until then, it'll be touch and go."

"I need to go back to the Maes headquarters," I heard Vicken said through the strange rushing sound that filled my ears.

"You can't leave me with them. If you do, I'll throw them out on the street."

"But they'll die!" Vicken's anguish words pushed into my fading mind."

"Then you better stay and help me." The last thing I heard was the man mutter, "Help from a vampire. The world has truly come to an end."

It felt as though only seconds had passed before my eyes agreed to open again. I closed them quickly at the brilliant light that surrounded me. I strained my ears to hear if anyone was around, but by the sound of things, the only talking was coming from a different room. I opened my eyes slowly and waited for them to adjust to the brightness.

Glancing up, I saw dozens of mirrors aiming light down from a hole in the ceiling. It wasn't a domed skylight or windows, there was an actual hole, and through it streamed moonlight that bounced off the angled mirrors to me. No wonder I felt so much stronger. Intermingled with the mirrors were crystals like those Dr. Six used to heal her patients quickly. Whoever this werewolf was, at least he was prepared.

I pushed up gingerly to a standing position and was pleased to find that the weakness was gone. Even though I was still in wolf form, I felt far more human than I had the day before. I could reason and my thoughts were at least in words instead of just images. I took several deep, testing breaths. My heart beat regularly with only the faintest tremor. I stretched and felt the tightness of my muscles release. I felt better than I had since being shot by the first set of bullets.

I jumped down from the table and landed lightly on the floor. Away from the blinding light, I could see the reason for Vicken's initial disgust. Leaves, even branches, and plenty of dust covered everything in the room. The cabinets in the corners were piled with newspapers, books, trinkets, and boxes that didn't look as though they had been opened in years. At the far end of the room was a couch with a pile of freshly disturbed newspapers scattered around it. The couch and the table on which I had been lying were the only big pieces of furniture I could see.

I caught movement out of the corner of my eye. Following the motion, I spotted a small demon. My gaze moved from it to another, and another. Demons lounged on the clutter and debris. Fortunately, they didn't appear the least bit interested in me. When I padded past them, they didn't even blink, but the fire in the depths of their eyes made me move faster.

"But the physics don't make any sense."

The sound of Dara's voice sent me wandering down the hall. The clutter from the first room continued, spilling out onto every available surface. Each corner was filled with stacks of newspapers, doorways were clutters with clippings of articles taped and pinned, and books of every size and shape were stacked down the middle of the hallway. And in each place, demons also sprawled as if they had been there for a while. It was unsettling. I had to squeeze my way past several stacks of demon-topped newspapers before I reached the source of the voices. The last stack, an impressively massive array of tomes that appeared to be older than the house, let off a cloud of dust that clung to my nose. I sneezed before I could stop myself.

"Finn?" Dara called.

Footsteps rushed across the floor. I fought back the urge to grin at the sight of my friends when they appeared in the doorway.

"Oh, Finn!" Dara exclaimed.

She fell to her knees and hugged me tight. I glanced up at Vicken. The vampire leaned against the doorframe and crossed his arms with a pleased expression on his face.

"Good to see you up."

I wanted to thank him for his desperate race to help me, but couldn't say anything in wolf form. Frustration at being stuck filled me. The thought of being human danced elusively at the edges of my mind. I wanted to grasp it, but couldn't with the moonstone in my shoulder.

"Come on," Dara said. "You need to meet someone."

I padded into what turned out to be the kitchen of the chaotic house. Similar piles took up most of the counter space, but it looked as though the table had been recently cleaned off. At the far end sat a strange individual.

"Finn, this CJ. CJ, meet Finnley Briscoe."

The man's eyes narrowed when they met mine. I could barely see them through the man's long, tangled, dirty-blonde hair and thick beard. There was no way to tell where his hair, his mustache, or his beard began or ended because they all flowed together in one matted, ratty mess. He looked as though he had never seen a razor or a comb in his life.

His clothing wasn't much different. The shirt he wore was tattered and a color of brown I guessed it hadn't been when it was bought, or found in an alley. The glimpse of his legs I could see beneath the table showed the same worn work boots I had seen when he carried me into the house. His pants may have been jeans once, but were covered in layers of dirt and unknown substances to the point that they appeared almost as brown as his shirt.

I nodded my head in greeting with the reminder that I owed this man my life.

The man nodded back and gave a grunt. "Why are you still a wolf? It's considered rude to remain in wolf form when you're a guest unless it's a full moon." He stretched his arms in front of him. I realized with a start that he was wearing a tee-shirt, not a long-sleeved shirt like I first thought; his arms were just that dirty. "And I can tell it's not, so don't be rude. There's extra clothes in the bedroom." He paused, then said in a slightly embarrassed voice, "They might not be clean, but they'll work."

When I made no move to follow his suggestion, he glanced at my friends. "What's wrong with him? Is he slow or something?"

"No," Dara said quickly, coming to my defense. "Something must be wrong." She reached a hand out toward me. "Show me, Finn."

The memory of her collapsing when she touched me on the porch was still heavy in my mind. I backed away before she could reach me.

"Maybe he likes being a wolf," CJ said with a grunt. "It's easier. You don't have to worry about politics, human thoughts, or memories." His voice tightened. "Sometimes I spend months here as a wolf. Trust me. You're better off leaving him alone. He'd rather be an animal."

"No," Dara denied, "He's not like that. Something's wrong. I know it!" She turned to me, her gaze pleading, "Finn, show us what's wrong. It won't hurt me, I promise."

At my uncertainty, Vicken spoke up. "If you don't show us, how are we supposed to save your baby sister?"

Out of the corner of my eye, I saw CJ sit up slowly. "He has a baby sister?"

Vicken nodded with his gaze still on me. "Finn's parents were kidnapped by the Maes. His sister was born there. He got his parents back out, but she's still there. We have to get her out."

The thought of the newborn sister I had never seen trying to survive in the clutches of the Maes made anger burn through my body. I stepped forward, determined to get back to human form so I could do whatever it took to rescue her.

"You'll show me?" Dara asked.

I took a hesitant breath, then nodded. Her hand settled gently on my head and she closed her eyes. Vicken's hand was a reassuring pressure on my back.

"Don't worry. If anything happens to Dara, I'll stop you," he promised.

I was about to close my eyes when CJ rose from the table. He crossed toward us, his aroma of dust and filth thick enough that I had to stifle another sneeze.

"Let's see what we're working with," he said in a grumble before he set his hand on my shoulder.

I closed my eye, found the painful memory, and pushed it at them.

The wolf side of me hated showing myself at my weakest. Chained to Sir Harbrand's table, my heart feeble enough that he could hold me down with a hand on my bare chest, I watched again as he put the scalpel to my shoulder. I heard Dara's swift intake of breath at the feeling of blood running down my skin. Sir Harbrand's bandana hovered in front of my face as he worked the moonstone into the wound below my collarbone, then he looked up again with triumph on his face.

My body began to phase. I watched myself struggle to attack them, but the impact of the bullet knocked me to the floor. I pulled the memory away as Edgart slipped the muzzle over my face.

"What was that?" Vicken asked, his voice tight.

"A moonstone," CJ replied. He had backed away to stand near the hall. His arms were crossed in front of his chest and he regarded me warily. "Those Maes aren't fooling around, I'll give them that. It'll keep him in wolf form until it's removed. The effects of a moonstone can make it hard for him to remember what it's like to be human. Do you have that problem?"

I nodded at the reminder of the day before when I couldn't understand what anyone was saying at the headquarters. I didn't want to fall back into being a complete wolf. The thought terrified me beyond words.

"So can you remove it?" Dara asked.

CJ shook his head quickly. "What do I look like to you, some sort of doctor?"

"Anything but," Vicken muttered.

CJ nodded. "Exactly. You really want me operating on your friend?"

"But we don't have time to go back to Haunted High," Dara replied. "There's no way his sister has time for that. You're the only hope he has!"

"Then he's in worse trouble than if you'd never come here," CJ replied. He left through the door and disappeared down the hall.

Dara and Vicken stared at each other.

"What was that?" Dara asked.

"Maybe he's scared," Vicken replied.

"Of course I'm scared," CJ yelled from further down the hallway. "I'm terrified! As you both should be!" He muttered something about being overrun with teenagers, then shouted, "Give up. Leave your friend a wolf and get out of here. He'll be better off than messing with that lot again."

Tears glimmered in Dara's eyes when she said, "But what about Amelia?"

Any sounds from the hallway ceased. We waited in silence until CJs footsteps returned at a much slower pace.

"Is that the baby's name?" he asked, his voice reluctant as though he didn't want to know.

"Yes," Dara replied. I could feel her pushing toward him, willing him to join us. "And we can't leave her there. She deserves to be home with her family, loved and cared for as a baby should be." She looked back at me. "Finn won't give up, even if he's stuck in this form. He'll get himself killed trying to fight them himself, and I won't let him go alone."

"Me, either," Vicken said from behind me. "So if you don't remove the moonstone, the three of us are still going back to the Maes headquarters, and if we die, it's on your head."

"My head?" CJ replied. "I didn't even know you guys until yesterday. This is ridiculous!"

"Well, that's just the way it is," Dara said.

CJ didn't look as though he was going to budge. Even though I knew it was a death sentence for the three of us, I rose and made my way past him to the front door. I stood there facing the door until Dara and Vicken joined me. When the werewolf didn't try to stop us, Vicken put a hand on the doorknob.

"Fine!" CJ said in a strangled shout. "Fine, but I can't guarantee anything!"

I held back a sigh of relief when I turned around. A glance up showed a smile on Dara's face. She winked at me. It made me wonder how hard she had been pushing acceptance toward the strange man. She looked triumphant and exhausted at the same time.

"We need to use the kitchen to operate," CJ said when we joined him in the cluttered hall.

"What about the moon room?" Vicken asked.

"The last thing a moonstone needs is more moonlight. Let's clear a place," CJ replied.

"Easier said than done," Vicken muttered with a glance around the room.

Since I was too big for the tiny round table, it was decided that the best place to operate would be the floor. Dara didn't let me lie down until Vicken had moved everything within reach and she swept it.

"Do you have a mop?" she asked CJ.

He gave a short chuckle as if she had told a joke, then at the realization that she was serious, he shook his head. "We're just going to have to make due. If Finn gets an infection, it's his fault for coming to my house in the first place."

At that reassuring thought, I settled down and rolled onto my side.

Vicken held out the jar of knives he had cleaned in the sink and then proceeded to soak in the vodka he had pulled from the freezer, much to CJ's chagrin and muttering about a waste of a perfectly good beverage. Dara stood ready with several towels she had scrounged from the truck. It was an unspoken agreement between us that nothing from the house would be used to stop the bleeding until I healed. Vicken poured the remaining contents of the bottle over my shoulder until CJ stopped him.

"Save some for after. He might need it for the pain," he said.

The three of us exchanged looks of doubt that any of what remained would be used for me.

Chapter Eleven

CJ LEANED OVER ME with a small steak knife. By the looks of the serrated edge, this was going to hurt far worse than the scalpel. Vicken put his hands on my shoulder and side, ready to hold me down if the pain became too much.

"Ready for this?" CJ asked.

For the first time, I saw concern in the man's eyes. He watched me closely, his brows pulled together beneath his shaggy hair. When he lifted the knife, I noticed that his fingers trembled slightly. With the thought that it was either him or my friends, I closed my eyes and nodded. At the very least, I didn't want my friends to carry the memory of slicing me open.

CJ parted my fur, and then grunted. "Looks like I have to remove some staples first. Too bad this thing's healed already." He held out a hand. "Butter knife."

Vicken gave it to him without a word.

CJ slid a butter knife under the first staple and pulled up. Having the staples removed wasn't my favorite moment, but the thought of what was to come made me remain still. "Five, huh?" CJ muttered when he was done. "Seems like a bit of overkill on a werewolf, but alright. Let's begin again." He picked up the steak knife.

Dara grabbed my paw as CJ sliced into my skin. It took all of my willpower not to jerk away from the pain.

"Breathe," Dara whispered into my ear.

I felt her pull and heard the way her breath caught. I opened my eyes and was met with her tight smile.

I wanted to tell her not to take my pain. It wasn't right that she was so ready to help me when everyone else in her life had been so cruel. I had told her before that I never wanted her to take my pain on herself, yet here she was, helping to ease me through the surgery.

"It's alright," she whispered as though she saw the argument in my gaze. "It's easier when I'm not the one under the knife. Trust me."

CJ cut deeper and we both sucked in a breath. Dara squeezed my paw. I kept my gaze on her beautiful violet eyes.

"Almost there," CJ muttered.

"Hurry," Vicken said.

CJ glared at him. "You want to do this?"

Vicken shook his head quickly. "I'm just worried about his heart."

The anger in CJ's face faded and he turned back to the wound. "One more second."

I grunted as the knife bit deeper. Dara's hand trembled.

"There!" CJ exclaimed. He pulled the moonstone free and threw it across the room. At everyone's astonished looks, he shrugged. "I don't want to be a wolf forever, either."

He rose. "Well, that was fun."

Dara stared from me to him. "Aren't you going to close it so he's not bleeding?"

CJ shook his shaggy head. "I told you I'd remove the moonstone. You can deal with the rest." He left the room without a backwards glance.

"Did he really just do that?" Vicken asked. His face was paler than usual. I noticed him glance at the bleeding wound and then away. "I would help, but I really can't."

Dara must have seen his glance, too, because she said, "It's alright. I'll take care of it."

Vicken quickly left the room. I followed the sound of his footsteps as he followed CJ. Their voices were quiet when he asked, "Are you alright?"

"Yeah," CJ replied. "I've just never cut someone open before. It's one thing to kill and eat when you're a wolf, but another by far to slice through skin and see someone bleed on your kitchen floor. I guess I just wasn't prepared."

"Me, either," Vicken said.

"How so?" CJ's voice was tight as though he needed some reassurance.

Vicken was quiet a moment, then he said, "Have you ever felt the urgent need to drink your best friend's blood?"

CJ gave a little chuckle and replied, "Nope. I haven't had that one. I guess you win."

"Yay, me," Vicken said drily.

"I'm sorry," Dara whispered.

I realized there were tears in her eyes as she used one of the towels to clean around the wound.

I wanted to tell her it was alright. Apparently, that one thought was enough to remind my body what it felt like to be human. In the most uncomfortable setting I could imagine, I began to change back to human form.

"Are-are you phasing?" Dara asked. "Right now?"

I tried to stop it, but I couldn't. It felt as if my body had been as anxious to get rid of the moonstone and phase back as I was. I only wished it had given me a little more warning.

Dara's eyes widened and she backed away to give me my space. The moment I was able to, I grabbed one of the towels and wrapped it around my waist. The end of the phase found me sitting back in my human form clutching at my towel in an attempt to maintain some modicum of modesty around the girl I loved.

"Are you alright?" Dara called from where she crouched on the other side of the kitchen table.

The hilarity of the situation struck me and I began to laugh. Answering laughter came from Dara as she rose and walked around the table toward me. I leaned my head in my free hand and laughed until I could barely breathe. Dara held a towel to my wound and laughed beside me until we were both left grinning and exhausted.

"Oh, my goodness," she said, wiping away tears from her eyes. "I haven't laughed that hard in a long time!"

"You should have seen your face," I replied, chuckling even though my ribs hurt from laughing so hard. "You had the cutest, panicked, 'Is he going to phase right here' look going on!"

She grinned. "It's pretty ridiculous."

I nodded, glancing around. "This isn't the situation I would have chosen for you to see me like this."

Her grin widened and she said, "I changed your clothes at Vicken's mansion, remember?"

"So why were you so quick to leave when I was phasing," I challenged teasingly.

Dara's eyebrows rose. "Well, it's different when you're awake." Before I could tease her further, she said, "Let's get you stitched up before you bleed through these towels."

"Yeah," I replied. "The last one is currently being used."

She removed the needle and thread from the cup of vodka and held it up. "Ready?" she asked with an uncertain expression.

"Ready," I replied.

She was about to poke me when I caught her hand. "No pulling this time."

"I don't know what you're talking about," she said innocently.

I gave her a straight look. "You can't stitch me up and share my pain at the same time. I can handle it."

"Are you sure?" she asked.

It wasn't like we really had a choice. I nodded with my most confident expression plastered on my face. "Stitch away."

By the time she was done, I was tempted to drink from the nearly empty bottle at my side. But the thought of what we had left to do kept me from reaching for it. Dara used the last of the vodka to clean up the blood that had dripped down my shoulder, then stood back to survey her work.

"Done," she said with an approving nod.

"Thanks," I replied. "We were sort of left hanging there."

"Sort of?" she shot back. "They turned tail and ran."

I thought of CJ's shaken voice when he said he had never cut someone open before. "At least the moonstone is out. I'm grateful for that."

"Good riddance," CJ replied when he and Vicken walked back into the kitchen. "You can take it with you when you leave. I want that thing as far away from me as it can possibly be."

"We will," Dara promised. She eyed the small, bloody rock that sat innocuously in the corner. "But, uh, do you have an idea how we can carry it without it affect us? I'm not sure what it'll do to Vicken and me. Finn definitely doesn't need to phase again."

We met each other's eyes with matching grins at the thought.

"I have a box here somewhere you can use," CJ said. "I'll have to find it, though." He gave me a disapproving look. "And you should go get dressed. Standing like that in front of a lady isn't appropriate. There's clothes in the bedroom down the hall. You're welcome to whatever you can find."

"Thanks," I replied.

When I left the kitchen, I heard him say, "The kid's got a lot of scars. What happened?"

"He fought demons at the Academy," Dara said.

"And in the city," Vicken seconded.

"Oh, and don't forget those demon-possessed mountain lions," Dara added.

I rolled my eyes and opened the door to the bedroom at the end of the hall. Any hopes I'd had that it would be cleaner than the rest of the house vanished at one glance. I stepped gingerly inside.

"And the bear," I heard Vicken continue.

"There was a bear?" Dara asked with horror in her voice.

"That's why we jumped into the river in the first place," Vicken said. "Before the mountain lions."

"Anything else?" CJ asked. I couldn't read the emotion in his tone.

"There was the demon in the corridor," Vicken said. "That's the one that burned his hand."

"And the Demon Knight. Not to mention the Wiccan Enforcer. She nearly killed him before she died," Dara told him as I pulled on a pair of sweat pants I spotted in a corner.

I found a shirt in a pile of clothes that had been tossed on the floor. It smelled a little stale, but better than the rest of the heap.

"He fights demons?" CJ asked.

"And runs from them," Dara said with a laugh.

No laugh came from Vicken, though. I knew he was remembering the one that bit his leg. He almost hadn't survived that one.

"And they teach you all of this at the Academy?" CJ asked with disapproval in his voice.

"Oh, no, not to everyone," Dara replied. "We're part of a defense team for Haunted High. With all of the demons around lately and…."

My eyes locked onto a picture on the nightstand near the bed and the sound of Dara's voice faded away.

It was the only clean thing in the room. Where everything else was covered in a deep layer of dust, the picture was spotless; a circle of space surrounded where it sat on the nightstand as if CJ didn't let anything near it.

I picked up the frame. A closer looked confirmed what my first glance had shown. I sat on the bed without a care for how the movement made mice squeak beneath the mattress.

Mom's face looked back at me from the photograph I held. She was younger than any of the pictures we had of her, but her carefree smile and the green eyes that matched mine were unmistakable. When she was older, she had always kept her wavy blonde hair combed out and free on her shoulders. In the picture I held, her hair had been plaited into a braid on either side of her head. She grinned at the camera with a smile that made me think of Drake, and she leaned against a boy who was a head taller than her.

My heart gave a painful thump when I looked into the face of the older boy and saw CJ's eyes looking back at me. It wasn't possible. It couldn't be. Professor Briggs had killed him after he attacked the school and slaughtered so many students and professors. There was no way the CJ who had just saved my life with the moon mirrors and cut the moonstone out of my shoulder was Conrad, my mother's brother who savagely attacked the school and had werewolves banned until I showed up.

I turned the frame over and removed the back. With shaking fingers, I carefully took out the photograph. On the back, the words, "Silvia Marie Roe and Conrad Justin Roe, ages twelve and fourteen."

I rose numbly and made my way to the door. With feet that felt weighed down by cement, I carried the picture out of the room and toward the kitchen. The demons that looked at me when I passed by suddenly made sense.

"This box is perfect!" Dara was saying when I walked in. "I can't believe you have an ironwood box. It'll block the effects of the moonstone so we can carry it!" She was quiet for a moment, then she said, "It matches the boxes Professor Briggs has."

"Ironwood is handy," CJ replied levelly.

"Why do you have an ironwood box that matches Professor Briggs'?" Vicken asked.

I saw the suspicion on his face. There was something about the vampire's gaze that said he was close to guessing the truth.

With a sick feeling in my stomach, I said, "Because he's been to Haunted High. He was a student there." I met CJ's gaze. "Weren't you?"

The man spotted the photograph in my hand and his eyes widened. "What are you doing with that?" he demanded.

He crossed the kitchen toward me. I backed up out of reach and hid the photograph behind me so he couldn't grab it. "You were a student at Haunted High, weren't you?" I demanded, louder.

"Give me that picture!" he yelled.

Tears burned in the corners of my eyes when I said, "I will if you tell us the truth."

CJ paused, his chest heaving and his hands still raised from trying to get the photograph.

"What's the truth?" Dara asked quietly.

I met CJ's green eyes that were so like my mother's and said, "Do you want to tell them or should I, Uncle Conrad?"

Dara gasped at my words and I saw Vicken nod out of the corner of my eye as if I had just confirmed what he had been thinking.

Conrad fell heavily onto a chair and buried his face in his hands. "You weren't supposed to come here."

So many emotions filled me that I couldn't settle on one. The reality of who he was had knocked the air from me as effectively as if I had been punched in the stomach. I sank onto a chair across from him. Shocked silence filled the kitchen.

"You died." I hated how strangled and pathetic the words sounded when they left my lips, but I was so confused. I didn't know where else to begin.

"I can't die," Conrad replied, his voice thick with self-loathing. "Not with *him* following every step I make."

"Who's him?" Dara asked.

Conrad spoke into the hands he had covering his face. "The Darkest Warlock. Chutka's last subordinate, if I understood what you told me earlier. He took over my body. He kept me alive." Tears leaked out from between the man's fingers when he continued, "Trace thought he killed me. He should have, too. With the lives of all those students on my hands, all those professors, I should have died." His last words were high and agonizing when he said, "Why didn't I die?"

His confession shocked me. I looked up to see the same horror reflected by Dara and Vicken. I didn't know what to say and neither did they. We had lived in the aftermath of Conrad's actions. The terror he had inflicted on Haunted High had nearly destroyed the school. Even so many years later, the effects of Conrad's actions showed in the distrust I caught on the faces of professors and students. We were still fighting the demons who escaped when Conrad first opened the door to the realm of Chutka the Shambler. He had hurt so many people with his actions.

Yet, sitting there across the table from him, I knew I looked at a broken man. The sorrow in his eyes didn't match how I thought a killer should appear. His shoulders shook in soundless agony and the tears that rolled down his cheeks and were lost in his beard were real. I could feel his pain even without Dara's ability.

As if she read my thoughts, Dara walked over and set a hand on my uncle's arm. He turned away from her, but she merely moved her hand to his shoulder. She closed her eyes, and I felt her pull. Conrad's silent sobs slowed. His shaking eased and the tears stopped. But the aching in his eyes didn't lessen.

"The Darkest Warlock used my body to kill them. I felt him break those children and toss them aside. He used my werewolf abilities to tear through the professors as if they were putty. I couldn't stop him. I tried. I tried." His words faded to a whisper. "I should have been stronger." His green eyes, so like my mother's, stared unseeing at the wall across from him. "I shouldn't have meddled with the gate and unlocked things I didn't understand. I should have been able to stop him. It was my fault. It was all my fault."

"You were eighteen." Vicken's voice broke the silence after Conrad's words like a stone thrown at a pane of glass.

Conrad turned to look at him as if what the vampire said held some unseen power.

Vicken's yellow gaze was steady when he continued with, "You were only a year or two older than us."

"I should have been strong enough," Conrad repeated in a voice just above a whisper. "I shouldn't have opened the gate. I-I was tired of being stuck. I was mad that we had to hide what we were from the world." He looked at me. "I was tired of being a monster."

His words gripped my heart in a tight fist.

He turned his head back toward Vicken. "I was so angry at the way the world made us feel."

"You don't think I've been angry?" Vicken replied with steel in his voice. "You don't think I've wondered what it would be like to tear down those walls and expose monsters to the world for what we are? I'm tired of hiding!" Vicken's voice had risen to a shout. I didn't know if he was even aware of it. "You don't think being a vampire, a blood sucker, a thing to be feared and to hide from, a being who consists solely on the blood of others, you don't think I loathe my existence sometimes?"

Vicken's chest heaved as he and Conrad stared at each other.

Vicken blinked and his voice was quieter when he said, "You made a mistake, Conrad. You set something free you didn't understand and couldn't control." His voice was back to normal when he continued with, "You were eighteen and a student at a school filled with monsters who distrust and fear each other as much as the humans would fear us if they knew about us. You were angry and you made a mistake."

"A deadly mistake," Conrad said.

Vicken nodded but didn't reply.

I looked from Conrad to the vampire. I saw my friend in a new light. He had always come across as haughty and detached from the rest of the students. After seeing the mansions where he grew up and meeting his father, I thought I knew what it was that made him so distant. But I was wrong. Looking at Vicken now, I saw the anger he kept barely controlled, the fury at the life that had played him a bad hand. And I respected him all the more for the way he kept a level head and for the words he had spoken to the broken man before me, words that had given him back a shred of the humanity that had been lost in his eyes.

"How can I ever make it right?" Conrad asked, his voice a whisper.

"You help Finn save your niece, then you help us stop Chutka the Shambler from ever reaching this world." Vicken's gaze held his. "You end what you began and atone for the lives you took by making sure no one else is hurt by your mistake."

Conrad held still for several long seconds. The only sounds in the room were our breathing and the quiet ticking of a clock hidden behind the mountains of newspapers in one corner.

When Conrad let out his breath, it was with a rush of action. He rose and pointed to Dara. "Put the moonstone in the box." He glanced at Vicken. "Get the truck ready. Fill it with every newspaper you find in this house and tarp it off." Then he motioned in my direction. "Follow me."

I didn't know what to expect as I trailed my newly found uncle down a flight of stairs into a dark basement. My eyesight was just starting to shift to the grays of the wolf when he flipped on a light. I couldn't help staring.

Weapons ranging from samurai swords to fifty-caliber machine guns occupied rows upon rows of shelves. Where the upstairs was a grimy, muddled mess, the basement was organized without a speck of dust to be seen.

"You're going to have to change those clothes," Uncle Conrad said.

I looked down at the ratty sweats. "Glady," I replied.

He opened a big black box and pulled out a set of black and gray camouflage pants with a black shirt. "Put those on. There're boots on that shelf and socks in the box in the corner." He then threw me a bulletproof vest. "You're going to need that."

As I pulled on the gear, I watched him rush around the room with the air of someone very familiar with his belongings. He slipped bullets into a belt, slid clips into loops, attached what I realized with shock were grenades to another vest, and in the meantime handed me knives and clips to attach to my own. By the time I followed him back upstairs carrying additional vests that matched those we wore, I felt deadly to anyone who merely looked at me.

Vicken and Dara must have thought the same thing because they couldn't stop staring when we walked out of the front door.

"What kind of basement is that?" Vicken asked.

I shook my head. "You don't want to know." I thought of his rant and amended, "Well, maybe you do, but you probably shouldn't."

I handed him a vest and then helped Dara put hers on. Vicken had managed to stack every newspaper available in the back of the truck. The black tarp he had pulled over it made it look like some giant black beast waiting to pounce in the dark.

"Right," Uncle Conrad said. "Let's go." He set a huge gray nylon bag at his feet, then climbed onto the passenger seat.

At my surprised look, he said, "You're driving."

"I don't know where I'm going," I protested.

"I'll tell you," Vicken replied. "You're probably the only one here with a driver's license anyway."

I looked at the others. Dara and Conrad both shook their heads.

I climbed onto the driver's seat. "Somehow, I don't think a driver's license is going to help us if we get pulled over," I said with a nod toward my vest.

Conrad grinned. "At least it'll be interesting."

Chapter Twelve

"YOU HAVEN'T BEEN ABLE to rid yourself of the Darkest Warlock all this time?" Dara asked.

Uncle Conrad shook his head. "He followed everywhere I went, and his little minions, too."

He gestured out the window. I followed his gaze and heard Dara's breath catch at the sight of long-armed demons running alongside the truck with an ease that belied our speed.

"I locked myself in my house because I feel it's the safest thing for everyone else. At least if they're following me, they aren't hurting others, right?" Conrad finished with an edge of heartache to his voice. "It's my fault they're here. At least I can keep them away from others."

"What about the Darkest Warlock?" Vicken asked. "Do you see him, too?"

"I haven't for a long time," Conrad replied. "But I know he's there. I can feel him. He used some sort of spell to bind us together when I first opened the gate. I've read every book I can find on magic, but nothing says how to break a binding like that."

The heaviness of the weight he carried showed on my uncle's face. My heart went out to him.

"We'll find a way," I promised.

He gave me a small smile. "Don't make promises you can't keep, Finn. Your conscience will be less filled with guilt that way."

I held his gaze. "We'll find a way to destroy the Darkest Warlock and end this." I watched him a moment longer before I turned my attention back to road.

"I want to believe you," Conrad said finally. "But you've been dealing with the aftermath of what I did and I don't want to bring more down on your head. You guys don't deserve that." He sat up straighter. "After this, I'll return to my house with my demons, both literal and figurative, and you can go on with your lives." He waited until I looked at him. "That's the promise I want from you."

I refused to give it. The tension between us filled the truck until I felt Dara pull it away.

"Breathe," she said. "The demons aren't doing either of you any favors right now. The Darkest Warlock has to be secondary in this battle we're about to fight. Let's focus on rescuing Amelia. Everything else can come after. Agreed?"

I had to admit she was right. "Agreed."

"Agreed," Conrad said sullenly.

Not long after, the sight of the mall loomed into view. I gritted my teeth at the thought of going back inside, but I had no choice. I shoved my nervousness away and cleared my throat. "What's the plan?"

"Light the newspaper on fire, blow a hole through the doors, and drive on in," Conrad replied.

Vicken looked at me. "He is definitely your uncle."

"Dara and I will free the monsters from their cages and chains, and we'll track down my baby niece. Finn, you and Vicken distract the Maes leaders," Conrad concluded.

"How are we supposed to distract them?" I asked.

Conrad lifted a shoulder. "Figure it out. It's your only job and you're a werewolf. It should be fairly easy."

"Fine," I agreed. "But if you see Sir Harbrand anywhere, give him my regards."

A toothy smile spread across Uncle Conrad's face. "Will do." He looked up. "Stop here for a minute."

I did as I was told and halted us in the middle of the parking lot so that we faced the metal-covered front doors.

Conrad opened his door and climbed out, then unzipped the bag. To my amazement, he pulled out a bazooka.

"You brought a bazooka?" Dara said in shock.

"I've been dying to use it since I bought it," Conrad replied. "Let's see if it works."

He stepped away from the car and aimed the bazooka at the front doors.

"Here goes nothing," I heard him mutter.

He pulled the trigger and the rocket shot out across the parking lot. The explosion when it hit shattered every window I hadn't already broken. When the smoke cleared, it left us staring at a huge hole in the front of the mall.

Conrad jumped back into the truck.

"Go!" Vicken said.

I shoved my foot down and truck sped forward.

"Dara, light the newspaper," Conrad instructed.

Dara flicked the lighter she held and threw it into the bed of the truck as we raced for the mall. I watched the paper go up in my rearview mirror.

"Steady," Conrad urged.

The truck fit easily through the gaping hole. I slammed on the brakes and we slid to a screeching stop inside the main corridor.

"Right, everyone has their assignments. Meet outside as soon as you can," Conrad instructed.

He came out from the other side of the truck in wolf form. My heart skipped a beat at the sight. My uncle was a huge black and gray wolf with thick fur and huge fangs. I realized that was how I looked when I was a wolf. I had to admit that it was pretty intimidating. Sirens began overhead. Conrad took off toward the escalators with his nose to the ground. Dara grabbed his clothes was about to run after him when I caught her arm.

"You sure you'll be alright?" I asked.

She nodded quickly. "I'll be fine. You guys keep up the distraction; we'll free the monsters and find Amelia." She rose on her tiptoes and kissed my cheek. "Be safe, Finnley."

She took off after Conrad without waiting for me to reply.

"Let's go," I told Vicken.

We ran toward the escalators.

"Must be nice," he called over the sirens and the sound of the roaring flames behind us.

"What?" I asked.

He shot two guards who rounded a corner, then nodded in the direction Dara had gone. "Having someone care about you like that. It must be nice."

Warmth spread through me and I nodded. "It is."

He gave a confirming nod and fell in at my side.

I glanced over in time to see Uncle Conrad take down one of the guards. Dara then pulled something from the man's pocket and raced to the closest cage. Putting the key in the lock, Dara shoved the door open. The woman with long white hair and white eyes gave her a hug of gratitude. The two ran to the next cage.

Vicken and I raced up the escalator four steps at a time. Adrenaline pounded in my veins, the gun I carried felt comfortable in my hand, and my best friend was at my side. We were a force to be reckoned with.

It had taken less than a minute for us to break through the doors and race up the stairs. The Maes guards were in the middle of trying to figure out what was happening when we appeared at the top of the escalator. Vicken and I stepped off the stairs firing. In less time than it had taken to reach them, the guards were sprawled unconscious on the floor, the victim of Uncle Conrad's stun bullets that worked much like Mercer's in the Mythic Labs.

"More will be coming; we'd better hurry," Vicken said.

He shoved open the doors to the meeting room and we stormed inside.

"Don't move," I shouted.

Vicken swept to the right, keeping his gun trained on the men and women who stood behind the table where they had apparently crowded at the sound of the explosion.

"What do you think you're doing?" Madam Opal demanded.

"Shut your mouth," I growled. Her eyes widened when I aimed my gun directly at her.

"Finn, what's the plan?" Vicken asked.

It seemed like the worst possible time for him to ask, especially considering he always hated my plans anyway. But he was right. We had to do something.

I watched Madam Opal carefully and weighed our options. I could shoot her, I mean really shoot her, and end the threat she posed to the rest of mythic kind. I slid my other gun out of my holster and lifted it.

Madam Opal's eyes narrowed. "Go ahead," she said. "I don't think you have it in you."

"He does," Vicken said. His voice didn't betray how he felt about my decision.

My hand didn't shake and I knew my aim was true. I only had to pull the trigger. But before I could, my thoughts slid back to a memory that at first seemed random but made sense by the end.

Professor Briggs was a warlock with an ability to smell evil. In order to survive the Wiccan Enforcer, I had been forced to kill Dr. Fagrin and his two assistants.

Their deaths still hung over my head. The next time I sat in a class near Professor Briggs, I had asked him if I stunk of evil. Certain that my actions had sealed my fate, I waited for him to condemn me. Instead, he had replied, "Finn, you are the strongest person I know. You are selfless, kind, and would make the best Alpha a pack of werewolves could ever have." He had paused, then said, "And no, you don't stink, even if you are a werewolf."

Somehow, I knew that shooting Madam Opal, no matter what her crime, would make me stink of evil. I wasn't a bad person, and if she had chosen to be, I refused to let it change me. I lowered my gun.

"See," she said with a smirk. "I knew you couldn't do it."

A demon stretched from its seat in the corner. I glanced at it. Others lined the walls and casually watched the proceedings. Beneath the table, larger demons laid around as though waiting for something. A group of them were clustered around Madam Opal's feet. She didn't even appear to notice that her foot was merely inches from stepping on one. How would she react if she knew about their presence?

I crossed to Vicken with my eyes on Madam Opal's hands in case she went for her guns. I had seen her in action; the woman could definitely shoot and I didn't want to feel another bullet if I could help it. When I reached the vampire, I said, "Your fangs can suck blood. Does that mean they can inject it as well?"

Vicken glanced at me. "I'm not sure. I've never tried it." He waved his gun to indicate the room. "This doesn't seem like the time to ask."

I held out my arm. "I want you to bite me and inject my blood into Madam Opal."

Madam Opal's face paled and Vicken's mouth fell open.

"What did you say?" he asked.

I shot the woman a humorless smile. "I might not shoot her, but your father told me something that's stuck with me."

I watched the homesickness sweep through Vicken's gaze before he asked, "What did my father say?"

"He said, 'People who are cruel are also unpredictable because their acts of cruelty come from something deep and twisted inside. Look for the imbalance and use it against them. Fight fear with fear.'"

Vicken frowned with uncertainty until I gestured toward the demons under the table. His eyebrows rose. "You think if she has your blood, she'll be able to see them?"

I lifted a shoulder. "It's worth a try."

Vicken nodded. "It's definitely worth a try."

I held up my arm, careful to keep the other one trained on the Society members. He grabbed my arm, but gave me a searching look. "Are you sure you want to do it? You'll be sick."

I nodded. "I'm sure. If it works, it might make a difference."

Vicken sunk his teeth into my arm. My lips pulled back in a silent snarl at the feeling of the bite, but I didn't move. Vicken sucked in, then pulled free.

Madam Opal backed away into the corner.

"Don't you dare touch me!" she shrieked.

I couldn't blame her. The sight of Vicken with his drinking fangs elongated and blood on his lips from biting me was pretty intimidating.

Vicken didn't let her fear bother him. His ferocity when he grabbed her made me wonder how much he had been tortured when he was on display. He reached for her arm and she tried to slap him. In response, Vicken pulled her close and sunk his teeth into the side of her neck. The woman's scream rattled through the air.

Vicken let her go and backed away with a pleased smile on his face. "Enjoy that," he said. He turned his head and spit on the ground. I guessed it was to clear the taste of biting her from his mouth.

Instead of rejoining me, Vicken walked toward the other members of the Maes leadership.

"Leave us alone," a man shouted as he backed behind the others. "You can't stop us all. There are Maes headquarters like this one all over the world."

"I know," Vicken replied as he advanced toward them. "We might not be able to stop them all, but we can make a difference here."

With the speed of his vampire heritage and me doing the easy job of guarding the door, Vicken caught and bit every member of the leadership.

"What are those?"

I tore my eyes away from him sinking his teeth into the man who had used the others as his shield and looked at Madam Opal. She was backed into the corner, her eyes on the demons around the table. Those that had waited at her feet earlier were walking back toward her. Their long arms and legs worked spider-like as they closed the distance to her.

"Those are demons, Madam Opal. They feed on the scent of fear and pain that you've created here." I pointed to those closest to her. "As you can see, they know you're the source of their sustenance and they're grateful. They've been following you around since you joined the Maes."

Madam Opal's eyes were wide with fright. She pressed as close to the corner of the wall as she could, but still the demons advanced. They stopped only when they were inches from her feet and sat watching her with flames in their adoring black eyes.

"Wha-wha-what do I do?" Madam Opal whispered as though afraid to raise her voice any higher.

"They're all over the room!" a woman shrieked.

"They're everywhere!" another member said.

"Don't touch me!" the last man Vicken had bitten cried as he ran from two demons who followed him like maggot-filled spider creatures.

"Want to escape?" I asked them.

"Yes!" Madam Opal said immediately. "I'll call off the guards! You can all go free. Just get us out of here!"

"We're going to the infirmary," I suddenly decided.

"The infirmary?" Madam Opal replied. "Why the infirmary?"

"It's safe there," I lied.

I glanced at Vicken and was grateful when the vampire went with it. "Oh, yes, the infirmary is safe. We'll guide you down there."

"Th-thank you," Madam Opal said.

"Keep them away from us!" a man yelled.

"This way," I replied.

I pulled open the door. All of the Maes leadership members ran out without being told. To my amusement, the demons followed, anxious to feed on the fresh fear wafting from humans.

"What's the deal?" Vicken whispered when he reached me.

"We're going to see if we can kill two birds with one stone," I replied. "It might not work, but it's worth a shot."

"The demons?" he asked. "You're going to trap them like we did in Lark's basement?"

I shook my head. "I'm going to use them as bait." I gestured past the demons to the people who ran to the escalator.

"Bait for what?"

"Do you smell their fear?" I realized it was a ridiculous question since I was talking to a vampire instead of a werewolf. "Never mind. Help me inject as many guards as we can catch on our way down. The more fear we invoke in them, the stronger their smell."

"What's the goal?" Vicken asked. I could hear the frustration in his voice at me putting off telling me.

I gave him a grim smile. "We're going to entice the Darkest Warlock to come out and play."

"Finn," Vicken began.

I shook my head. "Now's our chance, Vicken. Let's at least try. You saw the look on Conrad's face. We can't send him back to that house filled with demons and we can't stop Chutka without the final piece of his heart. This is all related somehow. We just have to figure it out. Trust me."

I ran down the escalator to catch up to Madam Opal's desperate flight. Sweat was already beginning to break out across my skin as a result of the vampire's bite. I clenched my hands into fists and refused to show weakness to the humans. Relief filled me when Vicken fell in at my side. Each guard Madam Opal ordered to join us was quickly bitten before they could react to Vicken's attack. At their sudden ability to see the demons, the guards were more than happy to stay with the group.

By the time Madam Opal used her keycard on the infirmary, our ranks had grown to the size of a small army with both humans and several monsters we had freed from the displays. Panic showed on the faces of the humans around us and I could smell their fear. The demons played their unwitting part by following the scent, effectively herding the humans into the same big glass room where I had seen Sir Harbrand the first time.

"Are you sure we'll be safe in here?" one of the leaders asked.

"As safe as we can make it," Vicken replied. "It's your own sadistic ways that have gotten you into this position. We're just trying to help you get back out of it."

Madam Opal paused near the glass door. She eyed the horde of demons nervously. "How do we know these aren't hallucinations from the vampire bite?" she demanded. "I feel sick and dizzy since he bit me."

I took a chance and said, "If you can see them, you can touch them. Try it."

Madam Opal looked positively terrified at the thought. I couldn't blame her. The demons that waited at her feet swayed from side to side; they drank in the scent of her fear and gnashed their teeth for more.

Madam Opal reached out a well-manicured hand. Her fingers shook slightly as she stretched it out toward the closest demon. When the creature realized what she was doing, it stilled and watched her with its flaming eyes. Froth began to bubble at its mouth. My hand gave an answering throb. If the demon felt provoked, the froth would ignite. I had no idea what demon fire would do to a human. I watched, my muscles tense, as she bent down.

The instant her hand touched the demon, she screamed. In response, the demon's froth ignited into a roaring green flame. I shoved Madam Opal away and kicked the demon in a desperate attempt to get it clear of the others so they wouldn't spit fire as well. My werewolf strength came into play and the demon flew across the hallway, slammed into the opposite wall, and fell unmoving to the ground.

"They're real!" Madam Opal said. "Get to the back of the room! Stay as far away from them as you can!"

I had to give her a glimmer of respect for trying to protect the members of her Society.

"What's going on here?" a voice demanded.

I turned slowly around and had to fight down the urge to phase into wolf form and attack Sir Harbrand like he deserved. His eyes widened when he saw me. The walking boot on his damaged ankle and the bandages covering his hand made a smile spread across my face.

Vicken appeared behind the man with stealth and a speed that made the hair rise on the back of my neck. He grabbed the man's arm and a yelp of surprise sounded from him.

"Is this the one who stuck that moonstone under your skin?" Vicken asked.

I nodded, not trusting myself to speak.

Vicken's eyes narrowed as he looked the man over. "I recognize your bandana." He bared his teeth. "You mess with Finn, you mess with me."

Sir Harbrand cried out when Vicken bit his arm in a motion that was over in the blink of an eye.

Vicken spat on the floor. "I'm going to have to brush my teeth after this, Finn," he called over his shoulder.

"You'll probably need to do a lot more than that," I replied.

"Wh-what are those?" Sir Harbrand asked in a shaky voice.

Vicken grabbed his sleeve and pulled him toward the door. "Demons. Thanks to your little training arena and display, your group has created a very successful demon feeding ground." He shoved Sir Harbrand through the door I held open. "Now stay in there until we figure out how to fix the problem."

Sir Harbrand hurried to the back of the room with the others, which left Vicken and me staring down a mass of demons.

"You know the glass isn't going to keep them out," Vicken said, his voice tight.

"I know," I replied. "We have options."

"Which are?"

I glanced behind me. "They're trapped. The demons want to feast on their fear. We can step aside and let it happen."

Vicken considered my suggestion, then shook his head. "As tempting as that sounds and as much as they deserve it, they might just die of fright." His scorn at the weakness of humans was evident in his voice. "I might be a heartless monster, but even I can't do that to them. What's our next option?"

The sound of a baby's cry stopped what I was going to say.

Dara's shout rang out. "Finn, we're in trouble!"

She rounded the corner with Conrad in wolf form right behind her. The bundle Dara carried in her arms gave another cry. At least fifty monsters they had freed from the training grounds and displays followed close behind. Just as I was about to ask what the problem was, a dark form turned the corner.

"The Darkest Warlock," Vicken said in shock.

"Bingo," I replied.

Chapter Thirteen

THE DARKEST WARLOCK WAS huge. His head nearly brushed the ceiling and the robes of his dark cloak hung around him like shadows. He had three eyes and they each burned with green embers. His hands were claw-tipped skeletal bones like Alden's when the Grim stuck them in the moonlight, only there was no moonlight so deep within the Maes headquarters. The entire air around the Darkest Warlock writhed and shimmered as if his evil was too great to be contained. His hands made strange gestures as though he worked spells while he closed the space between us.

Uncle Conrad spun and placed himself between the Darkest Warlock and the monsters he had helped to rescue. He snarled; the sound reverberated off the glass walls.

"Dara, get behind me!" I shouted.

The empath ran past me with the other monsters following close behind. I caught a small glimpse of the baby in Dara's arms. My little sister Amelia's eyes were scrunched shut and she was sucking in a breath to let out another angry wail. I felt Dara push and the baby's frustration stilled.

"Everyone, go in the glass room," I told them. "Dara, stay behind the others. Keep safe!"

"I'll help," a girl with purple hair said.

"Me, too," the man with orange scales echoed.

Other monsters joined us, choosing to fight instead of hide inside. I waited until the others were through the glass door, then I shut it behind me. It might not keep out the demons, but I hoped it would at least slow the Darkest Warlock down if we couldn't stop him.

"Uh, do we have a plan?" the purple-haired girl asked.

"To kill the Darkest Warlock and not die," I replied.

She rolled her eyes. "You really need to work on your plans."

Vicken grinned. "I like her."

The Darkest Warlock and Uncle Conrad were in a standoff. The Darkest Warlock kept trying to get past him, but every time he moved, Conrad leaped to stand in his way. Each sweep of the Warlock's claws threatened to end his life. It was the bravest thing I had ever seen anyone do.

I really missed my team from the Academy at that moment. Lyris and Brack could have helped with spells while the vampires used brute force. I was sure Alden would have some suggestion that might keep us from getting killed. He was the smartest of the group. At the very least, we would have a fighting chance.

"What is it?" Vicken asked at my side.

I shook my head. "I'm out of plans." At his stare, I said, "I wish the others were here."

"What do we need?" he asked.

"A shield to protect Conrad from the Darkest Knight, another to block the room so the demons can't get to the humans," I replied. "We also need an army, preferably vampire, and a Grim to tell us what we're forgetting."

"I can make shields," a tall, balding man from the group Conrad and Dara had rescued said.

"Me, too," an older woman with missing teeth told us.

"And I can make an army," the girl with purple hair said. "Sort of."

She raised one hand. On cue, a dozen Vickens surrounded me. She grinned. "You said vampire, right?"

I passed a hand through one. "They're illusions?" I asked.

"Yes," Vicken replied excitedly. "But he won't know which one is me. Can you do Finn as well?"

The purple-haired witch nodded. "Coming right up."

She raised her other hand and illusions of me joined those of Vicken. I waved a hand and they followed. I snapped and they did the same a split-second later.

"As for someone to tell you what you're missing," Dara said from behind me. "It's this."

She pressed something into my hand before slipping back into the anxious crowd with the baby held securely in her arms.

"What is it?" Vicken asked.

I looked down at the ironwood box. "The moonstone," I told him. My heart rose and I couldn't help the grin that spread across my face. "Dara, you're a genius!" I shouted.

A yelp sounded from Uncle Conrad. I looked up to see him slam against the wall. He tried to stand, but his legs collapsed from under him.

"Shield him," I said to the witch. "Protect the others," I told the warlock.

Their familiar chants filled the air and a shimmering orb surrounded Uncle Conrad. The Darkest Warlock tried to reach him, but his hand couldn't penetrate the shield.

"Our turn," I told Vicken.

I pulled out my stun gun and ran toward the Warlock, firing shots as I did so. Around me, the other twelve Finns did the same. The bullets didn't have any impact on the Darkest Warlock. I didn't expect them to. They were merely a distraction to get me close enough to inflict some real damage.

I pulled my knives from my vest and swiped at the Warlocks' side as I ran by. He let out an angry, wordless roar and turned to face me. But with the amount of Finns rushing past him, his claws cut through thin air.

Vicken did the same on the other side. This time, the Darkest Warlock got close. His claws raked through the air inches from the vampire before my best friend whirled around at my side.

"It hurt him," he said with excitement in his voice.

"But not enough," I replied.

I could barely make out the nicks we had cut in his skin. His swirling black cloak covered the injury, and when I looked again, the knife marks were gone.

Vicken swore. "So now what?"

Unable to find us, the Darkest Warlock turned toward the glass room. The mythics in front and those inside with the humans cringed away from the angry glare. I heard my baby sister give a sad little cry.

"We keep going until we figure something out," I said.

Vicken nodded. We brandished our knives and ran back at the Warlock. I had to give the purple-haired witch credit. No matter how many times the vampire and I attacked, the Darkest Warlock couldn't get a lock on us. Vampires and werewolves ran everywhere, swiping, ducking, and spinning away. Every time the Warlock's claws swept through empty air where one of our illusions had been, he became even more upset. The sounds of wordless fury that emanated from his mouth rebounded off the glass and multiplied until angry howls were all we heard. At the very least, we were tiring him out. At least I hoped.

"Any ideas?" Vicken asked me on his next pass.

Even the vampire was gasping for air. Our efforts to distract the Warlock were taking a toll on both of us.

"He needs to be weaker. I can't penetrate his skin deep enough for the moonstone to take effect. He's too strong." Worry filled me. If we couldn't stop the Warlock, there was a room of helpless victims he would make short work of.

At another cry from Amelia, I redoubled my efforts. I made another pass, but my legs were tired and I tripped on the edge of the Warlock's cloak. He grabbed me before I could get away. As soon as he picked me up, the illusions disappeared.

The Warlock lifted me high off the ground so that he stared into my face. "Enough of your games," he growled.

His deep voice reverberated clear through me. I struggled to free myself from his hands, but he lifted me up and his bone fingers tightened. I gave a yell of pain when his claws pierced the vest and sunk into my skin. A smile creased the Dark Warlock's twisted lips at my struggles and he gripped even tighter.

I focused all of my strength on one of his hands. Channeling everything that made me a werewolf, I tried to pull his clawed fingers from my ribs. At my efforts, his grip constricted. My back arched at the pain and I yelled again.

"Hold on, Finn!" Vicken shouted.

Out of the corner of my eye, I saw the vampire grab a guard and bring him close. A dozen other vampires acted out his actions. To my shock, the vampire bit the man's arm and drank deeply. When he let go, his lips and chin were red with blood.

Vicken's yellow eyes were wild when he ran to the Warlock.

"No!" I protested, afraid I was about to see my friend killed.

Vicken took advantage of the Warlock's occupied hands to scale his side. He climbed as though the Warlock was a tree, using the cloak and one arm to swing himself up to the Warlock's wide shoulder.

"Feel what it's like to be human for a change," the vampire said.

He bent down and bit the Warlock's throat.

The Darkest Warlock's eyes widened and the muscles in his neck tightened so that they stood out like cords. I pulled one of my arms free, tore a knife from the front of my vest, and plunged it into the Warlock's chest. He gave an angry roar and his claws sunk deeper into my sides. With a yell, I pulled out the knife and shoved the moonstone into the hole.

The Darkest Warlock's eyes widened. Inside his gaze, I saw memories, memories of a dark room, flaming demon eyes, and a feeling of helplessness. Those memories were over swept by another where a dark form loomed. In its hand was what looked like a piece of black rock. The Darkest Warlock accepted it and I felt his powers multiply until the demons cowered at his feet, eager to be his followers.

The memory shifted again. I saw the Warlock use the heart to lure a young Conrad into opening the gate. I heard the chants Conrad used and felt the power he yearned to hold, power that the Warlock used instead to take over his body and control him. The Darkest Warlock then turned that power on the students. I watched in mute horror as he tore apart students and professors as easily as if they were the petals of a flower. He threw bodies aside and looked for more, drunk in the scent of fear and pain that he caused.

The Darkest Warlock killed a girl I recognized as Mezania. I ached at the sight of her fallen body. I watched Briggs' young self run into the corridor and stop at the sight. A girl ran up behind him. My heart slowed when I recognized my mother. Briggs told her to run, then threw himself at Conrad.

Later, broken and bleeding, Conrad's misshapen form limped through the streets of the city driven by a force beyond himself. Demons follow in his wake. Those humans who saw him in the darkness scurried out of the way and hid their faces from the sight they later convinced themselves was a terrifying dream. I watched the Darkest Warlock force Conrad to make the mirror room. He lay there night after night until he was aware enough to realize the nightmare in which he now lived.

The Darkest Warlock blinked and the memory shifted. I saw the Demon Knight and the Wiccan Enforcer as though they sat within a deep, flaming green pit. They reached for me, their hands tipped with serrated claws. Behind them, a dark mass loomed. I could feel Chutka the Shambler's presence more than see it. He was outraged that we had bested his subordinates. The presence vowed vengeance and death for all I loved. He would come for me.

Warlock's hands spasmed open and I fell to the floor. Vicken grabbed me and pulled me backwards. We watched breathlessly as the Warlock clawed at his chest in a desperate attempt to release the moonstone. The stone glowed brighter and brighter until I had to shield my eyes. A massive tearing sound filled the air along with a howl of agony. I looked up in time to see the Darkest Warlock's chest rip open around the stone.

His eyes locked on me and he said in a voice I knew wasn't his own, "I'm coming for you. Everything you know and love will be destroyed. The world is mine. You will be the first to feel my wrath."

I rose to my feet and clenched my hands into fists. "Go ahead," I replied. "I'll be ready."

The moonstone exploded with a flash. Everyone ducked away from the brilliance of the blast. When we looked back, the Darkest Warlock was gone.

Vicken started to say something, but the sound of retching cut him off. I turned to see Uncle Conrad still in wolf form. He retched without throwing anything up for a few seconds, his chest heaving and agony on his face, before he gave one final cough. A black object fell out of his mouth to the floor. He backed away from it.

"Wh-what is it?" the witch with purple hair asked.

Vicken and I advanced. "The last piece of Chutka's heart," I replied. Cautiously and with the vampire's help, I scooped it into the ironwood box without touching it. Relief filled me when the box was closed and the effects of the heart piece contained.

"That was unexpected," Vicken said.

"Look."

At the sound of Dara's voice, we glanced around in time to see the demons scurry away from the humans and monsters. They skirted wide around Vicken, Conrad, and I, then charged for the doors.

"Where will they go?" Madam Opal asked in a tight voice.

I speared her with a glare. "Wherever they can feed on pain and fear. They'll be back if you don't change what you do here, and now you'll always be able to see them."

She had the presence of mind to look ashamed and lowered her gaze. "The Society is everywhere."

I nodded. "I know. We can't stop them all."

She met my gaze again. "But you stopped one. I realize there are worse monsters out there than we ever imagined. Perhaps we'll turn our attention to demon hunting."

Her words surprised me. "Really?"

She nodded. "And if I have any influence, I'll work to discourage the other Society members from such rash actions as we've been taking here, though I don't know if they'll listen."

"Let me know if there's any way I can help," I told her.

"I will," she replied. She hesitated, then said, "If you have anything you need from me, please ask."

I looked at where the Darkest Warlock had been. All that remained was a charred mark on the floor.

"If you have more moonstones, we could definitely use them," I replied. "In ironwood boxes, of course."

She smiled. "Of course. All that I have is yours."

"Thank you," I told her.

She nodded and left us in peace.

Dara touched my arm. "Are you alright?"

I could feel the sticky places where blood clung to my shirt from the Darkest Warlock's claws, but when I took a breath, the pain was dull. I nodded. "Nothing's broken. The rest will heal."

Her smiled was filled with relief. "That's good, because there's someone here who wants to meet you."

She lifted her arms and I found myself looking into Amelia's baby blue eyes for the first time.

"Go ahead," Dara said with a warm smile. "She needs her brother."

"What if I do something wrong?" I asked as she set the fragile bundle in my arms. She was so tiny I was afraid to move. I thought she would cry when Dara took a step back and no longer pushed comfort toward her, but Amelia merely looked up at me and made a little mewling sound.

Vicken leaned over my arm to get a good look at her. "I heard her cry. How can such a loud sound come from such a tiny creature?" At my glance, he grinned. "At least she doesn't look like you."

I chuckled. "There's that."

"We did it," Conrad said. He came over to join us dressed in his clothes once more. "He's gone. I can't believe it." He rubbed his arms. "I don't feel him inside of me. It's incredible!" His eyes were bright when he continued with, "I can't wait to tell your mother what happened. Silvia will be so happy she might even forgive me!"

My heart slowed. I looked at Dara and Vicken. Dara nodded in unspoken understanding and set a hand on Vicken's arm.

"We'd, uh, better make sure the other monsters are alright."

Vicken cleared his throat. "Yeah, I owe that purple-haired witch a thank-you."

They hurried away.

"What did I miss?" Uncle Conrad asked.

I looked down at Amelia, then back up at my uncle. "Uncle Conrad, I don't know how to thank you for all that you've done. We couldn't have rescued Amelia without you, and I would've died if it wasn't for your mirrors and that moon room."

"Finn, what is it?" he pressed, his gaze searching.

I knew I couldn't put it off any longer. I swallowed and said, "Uncle Conrad, my mom died when I was four."

Conrad stared at me as though I spoke in a different language. "What?"

"She died," I repeated. I took in a shuddering breath. "She's not here anymore."

Conrad shook his head. He looked from me to Amelia. "But-but your sister. You said she's your sister."

"My half-sister," I replied. "Everything was so crazy. I-I thought you knew. I should have said something, I just—"

"Didn't have a chance," Conrad replied. His tone was strange. He took a step back from me, then another.

"But I have a younger brother, Drake. He's your nephew, too. He would love to meet you," I said quickly, hoping to stave off the look I saw in his eyes.

Conrad shook his head quickly. "I can't meet him. Not yet. Not like this."

"Wait," I said. "Where are you going? When will you meet him?"

"Later," Conrad said. He turned and walked away.

"Later when?" I pressed. Anger filled me at his sudden change of heart. "I don't want you to leave."

Conrad's steps slowed, then stopped. He glanced back at me and said, "You're a good kid, Finn, and I'll bet Drake's a good kid, too." He shook his head. "But I'm not a good person. I've done bad things and hurt a lot of people. I need to fix that before I'm fit to be around anyone."

Amelia stirred in my arms. I swayed from side to side and her eyes closed. She gave a little sigh.

"When?" I asked.

"When Chutka is dead," Conrad replied. "I'll meet you at the Academy and we'll defeat him together. It's the least I can do."

I nodded because it was the only thing I could do. With a heavy heart, I watched him climb up the escalator and disappear from sight.

A hand touched my shoulder. "Let's get Amelia home," Dara said in a gentle voice.

Vicken gave me an encouraging smile. "You'll see him again. He just needs space."

I let out the breath I had unconsciously been holding in the hopes that Conrad would change his mind. "Thank you, guys. You're right."

"After Chutka's gone, there'll be plenty of time to make up the years lost between you guys," Dara said.

"I know there will be," I replied. "I just hate the thought of him being alone right now. It doesn't seem fair that he's lived this long and survived so much just to go back to his place by himself."

"At least the demons won't be there," Vicken pointed out.

I nodded. At least there was that.

"Come on, Amelia," I said to my sleeping baby sister. "Let's go home."

Chapter Fourteen

DRIVING THROUGH CLEARY FELT like returning to life before Haunted High. The sun was just beginning to set and school-aged children played ball in their yards and night games in the streets. I remembered being one of those kids, so carefree and oblivious to the dangers of the world. I hoped that Amelia could grow up the same way.

We pulled up to the house in the SUV Don Ruvine had given us. The moment I turned off the vehicle, the front door flew open.

"Finn!" Julianne shouted.

Dad and Drake rushed out after her. Though she looked better than she had at the vampire mansion, it was easy to tell that her recovery was going to be a long one.

"Mommy's here," Dara whispered to Amelia who slept soundly in her arms. She gave me a warm smile. "You should take her."

I gathered the baby up carefully and waited until Vicken opened the door before I climbed out.

"Thanks," I told him.

"Anytime," he replied.

I crossed the sidewalk toward the others. Julianne's hand flew to her mouth when she saw the baby in my arms. Tears streamed down her face as she carefully took the bundle from me.

"Oh, Finn," she said with such heartache I couldn't help answering tears from filling my eyes. "Finn, how did you do it?"

I looked back at Vicken and Dara. "I had some help."

Dad pulled me into a hug without saying a word. Drake joined us, and soon Julianne had her free arm around my shoulders. Together, as a family, we cried for the sake of being together and the happiness of being away from a place of such horror. For a moment, it felt as though we were back the way we had been before Sebastian died and I became a werewolf.

A minute passed before I remembered that we were in our front yard and there were neighbors who would be watching and who loved to find juicy pieces of gossip to share.

"Let's go inside," I suggested.

Julianne nodded. "All of us," she replied. She smiled at Vicken and Dara. "You're welcome to join us for dinner."

"You don't…I don't…I mean, I can meet you guys back at the Academy," Vicken said.

Julianne's smile was warm when she said, "Any vampire friend of Finn's is more than welcome in our house. Please come in."

Vicken followed close behind me as Dad led the way inside.

Amelia stirred in Julianne's arms and then gave an angry cry.

"She's so loud!" Drake protested, covering his ears.

"She's hungry," Julianne replied. "I'm going to go feed her. Please excuse me."

"I'll take care of dinner," Dad said. "Take your time."

Julianne shot him a grateful smile. We watched her walk away cuddling the baby who had been stolen from her and was now back in her arms where she belonged.

"She's had a very long day," Dara said.

Dad nodded. "They both have." His voice choked off, then he forced out with his eyes shining in gratitude toward Dara and Vicken, "I don't know how we can ever thank you enough. Our family owes you so much."

"We're glad we could help," Dara said.

"Yeah," Vicken seconded. "Finn would have done it all on his own if we didn't insist." He grinned at me. "He's very stubborn."

"He takes after me," Dad said with a proud look in his eyes. He studied me with his brow furrowed. "Finn, are you alright?"

I nodded despite how queasy I felt. The feeling of dried blood on my skin wasn't my favorite. "I think I just need a shower if you guys don't mind. Will dinner be long?"

"I'll make spaghetti," Dad said. "Take your time. It can sit as long as you need it to."

"Thanks, Dad," I told him.

I was about to leave the kitchen, but the thought of Dad the way he had been at the training grounds stopped me. I saw him again in my mind, his eyes feral, his only drive to save Julianne. He had been starved, tortured, and chained like an animal. Yet here he was, offering to make spaghetti for my friends to give me time to collect myself.

I crossed to him and gave him a hug. I felt his surprise before he hugged me back. When I stepped away, I knew he understood my thoughts because he squeezed my shoulder. Tears that he didn't let fall showed in his eyes.

He let out a breath and said, "Go shower. We'll wait for you."

I made sure my friends were comfortable, then walked down the hallway. My parents' door was open. I peeked in to see Julianne changing Amelia's diaper and walking Drake through the process.

"Then you use powder to make sure she doesn't get a rash," she said, her voice filled with a mother's warmth.

"A rash would be horrible," Drake replied. "You should use more powder."

"That should be enough," she said. "And then after we dress her, I'll show you how to swaddle her so she feels safe." She bent down and nuzzled Amelia on the cheek. "We'll help you feel so safe and loved, won't we?"

Amelia gave a coo in response.

Warmth filled me and the knowledge that everything was alright with my family loosened the knots in my shoulders. I stopped in my bedroom to grab a clean pair of pants, then made my way to the bathroom. I locked the door and faced the mirror.

I tried to pull up the hem of my shirt, but it was stuck to the wounds along my ribs. I pulled harder and my breath caught in my throat.

"Come on," I whispered. I pulled again and tried to ignore the pain. The shirt pulled free from one of the Darkest Warlock's claw marks. Blood trickled from the wound. The shock of what we had survived began to set in. I felt as though I was going to fall apart. My insides shook and my muscles tightened as if readying for another fight. I had to take several breaths and will myself to relax so that I didn't phase and take off from the house without looking back.

"Calm down," I whispered. "Just calm down. It's over. Everyone's safe."

With trembling hands, I sucked in a breath and was about to pull on my shirt again when a knock sounded on the door.

"Finn, can I come in?" Dara asked gently.

I leaned my forehead against the door. My wolf side protested against me showing such weakness to anyone. I shook my head slowly. "I-I don't think that'd be a good idea."

Dara was quiet for a moment, then she said, "Please?"

I couldn't bring myself to answer.

At my silence, she said, "Finn, I can feel you. Please open the door."

Her words held me. I couldn't deny the way I was feeling without lying, and she would know. Also, I didn't have the strength to pretend to be fine anymore. Defeated, I unlocked the door, then sat on the edge of the bathtub and bowed my head to avoid seeing any expressions of sympathy.

"Oh, Finn," she said. She closed the door softly behind her, then took a seat next to me.

I couldn't bring myself to look at her.

"I-I don't know what's wrong," I made myself say. "I can barely breathe, and I can't stop shaking."

I held out a hand. I could feel it trembling without needing to look.

Dara's hand slipped into mine.

"Just breathe," she whispered.

Her lips brushed my ear in a way that sent a shudder over my skin. I held onto that touch, the warmth of her hand in mine, and the heat that pressed against me from where she sat at my side.

"You've been through so much," she said. "It's a wonder you don't fall apart."

"I-I think I am falling apart," I admitted with a half-sob, half laugh. I looked at her with my head still bowed. "I don't know what's wrong with me. And I can't get this stupid shirt off!"

"You've been strong for everyone else. You just took down one of the biggest threats to mythic kind we know of, and that's after dealing with the Mythic Labs. Finn, you take care of everyone and protect them. Now it's time to let someone else take care of you."

Dara turned on the faucet behind us. I heard her adjust the water until she was satisfied with the temperature, then she pulled the lever to turn it to the shower.

"Let's take off your shoes," she said.

She leaned down and began to untie the boots I had gotten from Uncle Conrad.

"You don't have to—" I began, but she cut me off with a soft kiss.

"Finn, let me do it."

I nodded wordlessly and watched her pull off one shoe and then the other, followed by my socks. After she was done, she held out her hand to help me stand.

"Come on," she said quietly.

In a haze, I allowed her to pull me to my feet. Without bothering to do more than kick off her own shoes, she stepped into the shower. When she held out her hand again, I took silently.

"We'll let the water do the hard part," she said quietly as she positioned me so that I stood directly underneath the stream.

With my head bowed, the water ran off my shoulders and back. For some reason the warmth made my body start to shake. Tears filled my eyes and flowed down my cheeks to get lost in the water. Images of my dad and Julianne kept flashing through my head. I heard Amelia cry and felt the bullets hit me. The Darkest Warlock would kill everyone behind me if I didn't stop him. I was one werewolf against a force so powerful I didn't know what to do. Yet somehow, against all odds, we had beaten him and saved our loved ones.

I couldn't get the shaking to stop. Dara wrapped her arms around me and simply held me. She didn't pull with her skill as an empath. She knew I didn't want her to carry what I felt. Instead, she stood there with her arms around my waist and her head resting against my chest without a care for the water that soaked her long ashen hair. I was shaking so hard I felt her shaking with me, but I still couldn't get it to stop. I felt crazy, shaking like I was cold even though the water hitting my back was so warm. But my body wouldn't listen, not with the images that paraded through my mind like some macabre movie.

"Breathe with me," Dara whispered.

She tightened her hold and leaned further into me so that I could feel and hear her breaths. Each one was level and calm, the sound steady like the waves of the ocean beating gently on the shore. I closed my eyes, lowered my head so that my chin rested on her soft hair, and listened.

Concentrating on her breaths helped to chase the memories from my mind. I listened until the sweeping in and out became my only reality. The water, the pain, the memories, and even the fact that I was wearing my clothes in the shower of my youth and that I held the love of my life in my arms faded to the background. Only the sound of Dara's breaths remained.

In and out. Simple, sweet-scented, life-fueling, mind-calming breaths. It stilled my soul in a way that no other sound had ever done. Even the ocean paled in comparison to Dara's gentle, centered breathing.

"I love you," I whispered into her hair before I even meant to speak.

Dara's breaths stopped for a moment. Her hands grew still on my back instead of tracing the circles she had been creating on my wet shirt. When she looked up at me, the emotions in the depths of her violet gaze threatened to stop my heart forever.

"I told myself I would never love anyone," she said.

Afraid I had ruined everything, I wanted to take it all back, to pretend like life was fine the way it was before, to act as though I hadn't just said the words that made her look at me with such anguish in her eyes.

She blinked and a tear trailed slowly down the side of her nose. I had to resist the urge to wipe it away.

"I never…I never wanted to give anyone that kind of power over me," she continued, her voice quiet. She shook her head and lowered her gaze. "When my own parents used me like some sort of battery to recharge themselves physically and emotionally after a night of fighting, it hurt me in a way I can never get over. They didn't care how it affected me."

She sniffed without looking up and said, "Children are supposed to be able to trust their parents, aren't they? A parent's love isn't conditional based on what the child gives back, right?" She met my eyes and my chest tightened at the agony on her face. "They only cared when they found out I was leaving to Haunted High."

Her shoulders began to shake. I put my hands on them in the hopes that I could give her some comfort. She closed her eyes, then opened them again and cried out, "Finn, they handcuffed me so that I couldn't leave. They forbade me from stepping outside our front door. They actually bolted my bedroom door shut, and then would sit outside of it so they could still draw on my skills as an empath."

Anger that anyone could treat a little girl that way made me want to track them down and teach them what happens to those who abuse children. Only the fact that Dara needed me calm kept me still. Her bottom lip trembled and a sob escape her. I opened my arms and she buried her face against my chest.

"I've got you," I whispered. "You can let it all out. I've got you. I'll keep you safe."

Her sobs tore right through me. With every shuddering breath, I made a vow that she wouldn't have to hurt that way again. No one would ever use her if I had anything to do with it. The wolf side of me flared defensively, determined to do everything possible to protect her.

I heard Dad's words in the back of my mind. "You'll learn someday that werewolves love with all of their heart. It's a rare thing in this world, and a gift. I was honored to hold such a precious gift in my hands."

I felt that love for Dara. It was all-encompassing, full, and so complete I felt as though I would shatter and fly at the same time. Even if she didn't say the words, even if she could never love me back in that way, my heart was hers forever. I knew we were young, I knew it was cliché to fall so hard so fast, but my werewolf blood didn't understand reason. I was head-over-heels in love with Dara Jade, and I wouldn't be coming back from it.

Instead of telling her, I merely held her. She wasn't in a place for such confessions, especially after what she had just revealed to me. I held her until her breathing slowed to match my own, until her shoulders stopped shaking, and until she put her hands lightly against my chest.

"I'm sorry," Dara said.

I gave her a warm smile with a hint of my own embarrassment coloring my cheeks. "I'm the reason you're soaking wet with all your clothes on in a shower."

She smiled up at me. "I pulled you in, remember?"

"I remember," I said with a catch in my voice.

Dara looked down. "Let's see if the water helped."

She slipped her fingers under the hem of my shirt and lifted. This time, my shirt slid up with only a slight catch of the wounds. She eased it over my head, then let it fall to the shower floor.

"Finn," she said with her gaze on the dark bruises and stab wounds that covered my ribs.

"I know," I replied. They ached, but for some reason I could barely feel it.

Dara picked up a bar of soap. Without saying anything, she lathered it underneath the water and began washing the dried patches of blood from my sides. It was the strangest sensation to stand there and let her wash me as though I was some invalid. I felt foolish not doing anything, but I wasn't about to stop her.

"Turn around," she instructed.

A small smile crossed my lips at her command, but I did as I was told.

"These are deep," Dara said with concern.

"They'll heal," I reassured her. "The moon should be up by now."

I could feel the calling warmth of the moonlight in my bones. I knew I should be beneath it letting it heal my wounds, but I didn't want to be anywhere other than where I was at that moment.

"You've got to stop running towards trouble," she said. "It's bad for your health."

"It's a habit," I replied.

That brought a laugh from her.

I turned back around and smiled down at her. "Dara Jade, you are the most beautiful girl I have ever seen in my life."

She gave me a teasing smile and said, "You're not half bad yourself, Finnley Briscoe."

I felt a pang of regret when she then turned and stepped from the shower. She smiled at me as though she knew what I was thinking.

"Finish your shower," she said. "Maybe we can talk some more under the stars."

"Deal," I replied. "But if that vampire joins us, I'm done."

She gave a light, musical laugh as she dried her hair with a towel from the stack Julianne always kept beneath the sink and said, "Me, too."

I heard her hand on the doorknob and told her, "You can grab some dry clothes from my room. I don't know how they'll fit, but you're welcome to anything in there."

Her eyebrows rose. "A chance to go through Finnley Briscoe's stuff? Deal."

She shut the door and I couldn't stop grinning as I lathered shampoo in my hair.

I was glad to see the claw marks had stopped bleeding by the time I finished showering. I dried off and pulled on my pants with the intention of grabbing a shirt from my room on my way back to the kitchen. The smell of spaghetti cooking made my mouth water. Nothing topped Dad's special seasonings when he made the sauce. Topped with a bit of cheese, his spaghetti rivaled anything I had ever ordered at a restaurant.

The sound of a baby crying in the next room reminded me that my family had become bigger. I used the towel on my hair one last time, then hung it on the peg over the door. I grabbed my wet shirt and pants from the shower floor, wrung them out, then made my way down the hall. I paused by my parents' open door.

"What's going on," I asked. "Is Amelia—"

I froze at the sight of Grayson standing in my parents' room with a gun pointed at my family.

Chapter Fifteen

VICKEN STOOD IN FRONT of Dara with an angry snarl on his face that showed his vampire teeth. Julianne held Amelia and was desperately trying to calm her while Dad reasoned with Grayson.

"Hello, Finn," Grayson said. He kept the gun on my family but turned to me. His eyes flickered down to my chest. "Looks like you've had a rough day."

"You could say that," I replied levelly. "What are you doing here, Grayson?"

Grayson gave a little, maniacal laugh. "You ruined everything for me, Finn. I thought I'd return the favor."

I took a step forward. "But what about honoring our friendship? In the treehouse, you said you knew I never meant for Sebastian to die. You were going to forgive me, remember?"

"Stay right there," he snapped. "And yes, I forgave you, and then what did you do? You burned my treehouse to the ground! Everything I worked on is gone. All of my plans, all of the tracking charts, the headlines, the proof that monsters exist. It's all gone! And now I have to start over."

I shook my head. "The Maes aren't hunting monsters around here anymore."

He spat when he said, "You don't think I know that? You don't think I know that you ruined everything for me? I was going to be somebody, to do something. I was going to kill monsters like you to protect this world."

"From what?" I shouted. The anger at seeing my family at gunpoint after all they had been through simmered just below the surface. Amelia let out a cry at the sound. I took a calming breath with the reminder that Grayson was the one holding the gun and continued with, "From what, Grayson? Monsters are people just like you and me. They're not trying to hurt anyone. They just want to survive in peace."

Grayson's eyes narrowed. "There won't be peace with monsters around. You're too…unpredictable." His eyes lit up as though he was proud of the big word. He continued with, "But you know the ironic part? I need a monster to get into the Maes." He glared at me. "And I know you ruined the Maes here, but there are plenty out there. Trust me. I know the locations. I wrote them down."

"Did I burn them up?" I asked, unable to stop myself from goading him.

His mouth fell open, then he shut it again and glared at me. "That's besides the point. I found it once. I can find it again. And this time, your baby sister's going to be the one I take. She's the one they want, anyway." He flicked his gun at Julianne. "Hand her over."

My dad moved in the way, shielding them both with his body.

"There's no way," Dad said.

"Over my dead body," I growled.

Drake entered the room saying, "Hey, Dad, the sauce is about—"

His appearance caught Grayson off guard and his gun wavered. I took advantage of his momentary lapse. Throwing myself at him, I hit the gun up just before he pulled the trigger. The bullet buried into the ceiling with a loud bang.

Amelia started to cry again. I grabbed Grayson's hand and twisted his wrist. He released the gun with a shout of pain. I slammed a fist into his chest, followed by one to his head. He fell unconscious to the floor.

Everyone stared at each other. With my heart racing, I released the clip from the gun, then ejected the bullet in the chamber and caught it before it could hit the ground. I set everything on the dresser.

"I'm really tired of guns," I said.

Dad gave a weak little laugh. "I don't suppose you learned that when you were twelve?"

When I shook my head, more relieved laughter followed. I reached down to grab Grayson's arms so I could haul him to the living room until we could figure out what to do with him, but Vicken stopped me.

"I've got him," Vicken said. The vampire picked up Grayson's unconscious form and slung him over his shoulder as if he carried bodies all the time. I realized with a bit of chagrin that it was becoming a usual thing.

Dara glanced at my parents, then said, "I'll help." She followed Vicken out of the room.

Drake stared from the gun to me.

"That was awesome!" he exclaimed as though we hadn't just been close to someone dying. "Did you learn that at the Academy?"

"Sort of," I replied.

"Cool," Drake said. "I'm going to see what Vicken does with him."

When he hurried down the hall, I called after him, "Tell Vicken not to bite Grayson! He'll probably catch something."

My fake grin fell at the expression on Dad and Julianne's faces when I turned back around.

"I'm beginning to think we should move," I said in an effort to break the wall of emotions they tried to hold back.

"My goodness, Finn," Julianne said. "That was so scary." She hugged me tight with her free arm.

"That was brave," Dad said. He hugged me as well.

I was beginning to feel as if hugs only happened after we had just survived something potentially fatal. It wasn't a good feeling. I cleared my throat and took a step back. "Okay, well, let's at least get a security system until we know whether Drake's going to be a good guard dog."

Dad shook his head and rolled his eyes, but to my surprise, Julianne started to laugh. The sound startled Amelia, who began to cry again. Julianne was laughing so hard she could barely stand. Her laughter had an edge of hysteria to it as if she had just been pushed beyond her limit.

I took Amelia from her arms and Dad helped her to the edge of the bed. Amelia stopped crying when I swayed from side to side in the motion she seemed to like. I couldn't help smiling at her inquisitive expression that made her forehead wrinkle slightly as though she was far older than a newborn. I held her close and enjoyed her nice, clean baby scent now that she was cared for as a baby should be.

I pretended to be occupied with Amelia while Dad comforted Julianne. The fact that Dara and I had just experienced our own small breakdowns gave me that much more sympathy for what my stepmother had been through.

"It's alright, Juli," Dad said as he rubbed her back. "It's over. It's all over."

Julianne's tears fell onto her hands. "I can't take much more, Stephen. I just can't."

"I know," he replied gently. "It's all finished. No one is going to hurt our family anymore." Tears showed in his eyes when he said, "I promise. Everyone is safe." He wrapped her in his arms and looked as though he wasn't going to let her go for a very long time.

When Julianne calmed down and sat back, she kissed my dad sweetly on the cheek. "Thank you, Stephen. I needed that. I really did."

"Me, too," he replied. "It's been a rough few days."

"That's one way to put it," Julianne replied with a small laugh as she wiped the tears from her cheeks.

Amelia gave a little coo, bringing their attention back to us.

Julianne smiled. "Finn, did you just say you wanted your potentially werewolf brother to be a guard dog?" she asked with only a slight tremor in her voice.

"Yeah," I replied. "I figured he should be good for something."

She shook her head. "Just when I thought you couldn't surprise me anymore."

I grinned. "That's what stepsons are for."

She rose and hugged me gently with Amelia between us. "You're the best stepson a mother could ever ask for." Her expression became one of concern when she looked down at my chest. "Do we need to take you to a doctor?"

I shook my head with embarrassment at their scrutiny. "It's nothing a little moonlight won't take care of. I think I'll head out back after we figure out what to do with Grayson."

"The police chief's wife is a teacher at the school," Dad said. "I'll give him a call." He winked. "I'll just leave out a few monster details. I'm sure they'll have Grayson booked in a psyche ward in no time."

"Good idea," I replied.

"Do you want me to take her?" Julianne asked.

I realized I was still holding Amelia. I was surprised how quickly I had grown used to carrying the baby.

"Yeah, she probably needs her mommy," I replied.

I handed her over and found myself missing her immediately. But the look on Julianne's face as she cuddled her newborn daughter was priceless. Dad smoothed Amelia's downy hair with his fingers; the look of pride that showed in his eyes made me smile. I turned away and headed back down the hall.

I stopped in my room and grabbed on one of my favorite shirts, a gray long-sleeved one with a faded beetle on the front. It used to be the one I wore when we had a chill-at-home day with the family. It felt comforting to slide it on, even if my ribs hated the action.

Determined to get some of the moonlight my body craved, I glanced in the living room.

"How's it—" I stopped talking at the sight of Grayson hogtied in the middle of the floor. He was on his stomach and his arms and legs had rope wrapped around them with another cord looping Grayson's neck. If he awoke, there was no way he was going anywhere. "Is that really necessary?" I asked.

Vicken nodded. "Absolutely. You won't let me bite him, even though he definitely deserves the after-effects, and after what he just put your family through, he should be as uncomfortable as possible." He grinned, showing his pointed canines. "Besides, when he wakes up, he's going to be pretty sore."

I chuckled. "It serves him right. I hope we never see him again."

"He's going to wish the same thing," Vicken vowed.

Dad paused at the door with his cellphone in his hand. "The police chief's on his way over. You guys should probably find a place to hole up for a bit. You're supposed to be at the Academy."

"You've got this?" I asked him.

He nodded. "I hate changing the story for the police, but the fewer monsters involved, the better for all concerned, especially if Grayson starts running on about vampires and we have Vicken sitting in the corner."

I glanced at Vicken and had to admit that he was quite obviously a vampire.

"We'll go out back. I need to get some moonlight anyway," I told him.

The three of us scooped up bowls of spaghetti on our way through. By the heaping servings everyone took, I wasn't the only one whose stomach had been growling at the smell.

"Man, your dad can cook," Vicken said when we found comfortable spots on the grass.

I stared at him as he sucked a strand of spaghetti through his teeth. "I honestly don't think I've ever seen you eat anything other than blood."

He nodded. "I usually don't. Vampires get everything we need from blood. If there's one thing I can say about the Maes, they had the good quality red stuff." He stretched, then realized we were both giving him unamused looks. He explained, "Eating food is really just for the flavor, and most things don't taste nearly as good as fresh blood." He paused, then said, "Although, if we're being honest, I do have a stash of Twinkies in my room at Haunted High."

Dara and I laughed.

"Seriously?" she asked. "That completely ruins the bad boy vampire imagine I have in my head for you."

Vicken grinned. "Seriously. It's fun to suck out the filling with my fangs."

I made a gagging sound. "Gross. Now Twinkies are ruined for me forever."

"Me, too," Dara replied. "Although it makes sense that a vampire's favorite food can be sucked dry."

Vicken nodded. "Yes, it does."

"What about Oreos?" I asked.

He shook his head. "The filling is too dry."

"Reeses?" Dara suggested.

He made a disgusted look. "You don't know what gross is until you've had your fangs stuff up with peanut butter. Trust me. Twinkies are the way to go."

Dad came out about an hour later. He carried Amelia in his arms and looked exhausted but satisfied.

"Chief Darson took my report and hauled Grayson away. He said we'll probably be called in to testify, but that's just standard procedure." He glanced back at the house and said, "He was concerned about my black eye, but I told him I tripped carrying groceries in and hit my face on the doorframe." He grinned at me. "Remember when that really happened?"

I laughed at the thought. "You had a shiner for weeks. Everyone thought you got in a fight with the flag football coach!"

His smile faded when he said, "Unfortunately, reality is a bit harsher than that, isn't it?"

The three of us nodded.

Dad sighed and leaned against the house. "I wish you guys didn't have to see that. The worst humanity has to offer is pretty ugly."

I chose not to tell him about the Mythic Labs. By the looks Vicken and Dara shot me, I could tell they agreed it was a good idea.

"Is Mrs. Briscoe okay?" Dara asked.

Dad gave her a grateful smile. "She is. She's resting right now." He held Amelia close. "It's giving me time to catch up with this little one." Amelia appeared perfectly content to be cuddled at that moment, and Dad was happy to comply.

"Thanks for the spaghetti, Mr. Briscoe. It sure beats the food we get at the Academy," Vicken said.

Dad shot me a concerned look. "Is the food bad?"

I shook my head. "He just really likes your cooking."

That made Dad smile. "Well, I'm glad. Eat as much as you can. We have plenty."

"I'm ready for seconds," Vicken said. He gave Dara a look. "How about you?"

Dara glanced down at her half-filled bowl, then at me and Dad. "Uh, yeah. I could use more." She grabbed my empty bowl. "I'll get yours. Stay and soak in the moonlight. I know you need it."

Dara was right. I rolled my shoulders and enjoyed the way my ribs hurt less. Even breathing deeply no longer hurt. I hoped if I stayed outside long enough, the claw marks would stop aching entirely. If I had something like Uncle Conrad's moon room, I would probably already be healed.

The thought of Uncle Conrad made me sad.

"Dad, there's something I need to tell you," I began.

Dad seemed to guess that this wouldn't be a casual conversation. He moved a lawn chair over and sat facing me. Amelia snuggled contentedly in his arms. Her little hand gripped one of Dad's fingers. He ran his thumb over it as he kept his attention on me.

"What do you need to tell me, Finn?"

I wasn't sure where to start. Everything I had learned at the Academy about Uncle Conrad was so horrible, and a lot of that I had relayed to Dad so he could understand why there was so much prejudice against me as the only werewolf at Haunted High. There was no way to make light of the situation. I figured saying it straight was best.

"Uncle Conrad's alive."

"What!" Dad jerked forward so fast Amelia's eyes flew open and her face screwed up into the beginnings of a cry.

"I'm sorry; it's okay," Dad soothed gently. He rocked in his seat and she settled back down. After watching his face for a moment, her eyes drooped shut again.

I gave him an apologetic look. "Sorry. I wasn't sure how else to say it."

"Where is he?" Dad demanded. His voice was soft and singsong in an effort to keep Amelia asleep, but concern was written in every tense line of his body. "If he's targeting the Academy again, I don't want you back there, any of you. I will—"

"He helped us save Amelia."

This time, Dad's eyes went so wide it was comical.

I fought back a smile. "He's not what you think at all, Dad. He's normal." I thought of the man's shaggy hair, the garbage collected in his house, and the artillery room in his basement. "Well, not exactly normally," I amended, "But he means well."

Dad watched me closely. "Isn't this the same guy that killed all those students and professors at the Academy?"

I nodded. "Yes, but he was possessed by a demon at the time, and it kept following him so he couldn't get anyone to help or else the demon would attack them, too."

It all sounded pretty far-fetched to me, and by the look on Dad's face, he felt the same way.

I tried a different tactic. "I almost died at the Maes headquarters." I lowered my gaze and ran my hand across the grass by my leg. "I was shot too many times by those electric bullets. It did something to my heart, and then that horrible Sir Harbrand put a moonstone in my shoulder so I was stuck as a wolf." I glanced up at Dad. Though I could read how many questions he had in his eyes, he kept listening and didn't interrupt. "Vicken took me to Conrad's and when I woke up in his moon room, I felt better, much better. He removed the moonstone so I could be human again. It's the same stone Vicken and I used to destroy the demon that had been following him."

Dad was quiet for a moment. When he spoke, I couldn't read the emotion in his voice. "I'm glad he helped you, but I don't think you should trust someone who killed people. He should be in prison, Finn."

I couldn't deny Dad's words. "I know." I sucked in a breath. "But he's family, and without him, ours wouldn't be complete."

Dad looked down at Amelia. "I'm grateful for that."

"But?" I prompted.

"But your mother didn't even tell me she had a brother, that's how bad it was." His gaze begged me to understand. "We need to respect her wishes, Finn. If she wanted us to know about Conrad, we would have."

"But she didn't know he was possessed—" I began.

Dad shook his head. "Please do this for me. Don't contact your uncle again. I don't want him here around our children, and if you see him again, you need to call the police, understand?"

There was no give on his face. I knew nothing I said could make him comprehend what I saw in my uncle. I swallowed and nodded. "I understand, Dad."

Amelia opened her eyes. When she saw that neither of us were her mother, she began to cry.

A fatherly smile crossed Dad's face. "I'd better change her diaper and get her back to Julianne."

I nodded and stood. Holding out a hand, I helped him to his feet.

"When you're ready, let me know and I'll drive you guys back to school," Dad said.

"Thank you," I told him.

I sat back down, then settled onto my back on the grass. The moonlight felt like a warm blanket and a cool breeze all in one. I turned my head at the sound of the others returning.

"How'd it go?" Vicken asked.

I looked back at the moon. "Not good. He doesn't want me to associate with Uncle Conrad anymore. He says he's a murderer."

"He is," Dara said as she sat down beside me. She set my bowl of spaghetti on my chest. "But he's also not." She shook her head with a sigh. "It's complicated. I don't know how anyone else could understand if they hadn't been there."

"He's going to have problems when he gets to Haunted High," Vicken said.

I nodded. "We'd better get going. Things could get bad really quickly."

Vicken rose. "As good as the spaghetti is, I'm a bit due for a drink, if you know what I mean."

Dara rolled her eyes. "We always know what you mean."

I smiled and led the way back to the kitchen.

Chapter Sixteen

THE MOMENT THE GATE shut behind us, I could tell something was wrong. I took off running and the others followed close behind.

"What's going on?" Vicken asked.

"Don't you hear that?" I replied. "Someone's shouting!"

"I feel it," Dara said. "There's lots of anger. We need to hurry!"

The door swung open when we reached the top of the stairs. I ran inside with Dara and Vicken at my heels. I slid to a stop in the entrance corridor.

Students filled the high-ceiling room and professors stood clustered near one end. I pushed through the crowd toward them. Headmistress Wrengold waited at the forefront. The pained look on her face made my steps slow. When a gap parted in the gathering, I saw why.

Professor Briggs held a man pinned to the wall by his throat. It took me a second to recognize who it was. Uncle Conrad had cut his hair and his beard. A few marks where he had nicked himself were covered with bits of toilet paper. He was wearing a suit that looked a few sizes too small, and his hair had as many cowlicks as mine, which made combing it rather difficult. My uncle's blond hair stuck out in every direction despite whatever mousse he had used to attempt to tame it.

"How dare you come back here after what you did?" Briggs demanded.

Conrad didn't struggle even though he should have been able to easily beat Briggs with his werewolf strength. The look on Conrad's face was one of dejected sorrow combined with suffocation at the grip the professor had on his throat.

I shoved through the rest of the students. "Let him go!"

Briggs looked back at me in surprise. "Finn?"

"Let him go," I repeated. "He's my uncle. I'll vouch for him."

The look of loss and confusion that surfaced on Professor Briggs' face ate at me. Slowly, as though he had to will himself to do so, Briggs lowered Conrad to the floor.

The professor couldn't bring himself to look at me when he asked, "Why are you vouching for this filth?"

"Because he saved my life when Vicken, Dara, and I went against the Maes and the Darkest Warlock," I replied.

"You stopped the Darkest Warlock?" the Headmistress asked.

I pulled the ironwood box from my pocket and handed it to her. "The last piece of Chutka's heart." Headmistress Wrengold accepted it, but knew better than to look inside.

"It's the last piece," she said. Her gaze turned to Conrad. "And you…you helped my students get this?"

It hurt me to see how hard it was for her to talk to him. I couldn't blame her at all. Conrad had killed her husband. Even if he had been possessed by the Darkest Warlock at the time, it was his hands and his face she no doubt saw when she thought of the Headmaster's death.

Conrad nodded. His gaze was filled with tears that leaked down his face unashamedly. "I did. But it doesn't change what happened."

"No, it doesn't," Professor Briggs said in a growl. His hands opened and closed as though he wanted to throttle the werewolf.

Dara walked passed me to stand beside my uncle. "Conrad was possessed by the Darkest Warlock when he attacked the students here. It wasn't him that killed them."

"Did he tell you that?" Professor Mellon asked.

"The Darkest Warlock showed me," I told her. I kept my face expressionless to hide the horror of that moment. "He tricked Conrad into taking the piece of Chutka's heart, then used it to control him."

It was clear by the shock on the faces of the professors how much Conrad's appearance had shaken them. The students around us were alarmed, but I knew it was more from the reaction of the professors than the knowledge of what was happening.

"How did you even survive?" Briggs demanded; his voice was a strangled whisper. "I killed you for what you did. You don't deserve to live."

"He does," I replied firmly. "Just as much as any of us do."

Conrad closed his eyes and his head hung low. "You don't have to stand up for me, Finn," he said in a broken voice.

"Somebody has to," I replied. I met Headmistress Wrengold's gaze. The loss she felt was clear. "I'm so sorry about your husband and the others who were killed, but you have to understand that Conrad didn't do it."

When I saw that my uncle wasn't going to defend himself, I held out my hand to Dara. "I need you to help me."

"For what?" she asked.

"I need to show them, but I can't do it to so many at the same time. Can you add to my strength?"

Dara nodded and took my hand. "I'll try."

"What are you doing?" Professor Mellon demanded. "This can't work. It's—"

Her words were cut off when I raised my free hand and shoved the memory toward them. It was harder without direct contact, but using the strength Dara pushed toward me, I felt the memory leave me and flow to them.

The images of Conrad under the Darkest Warlock's control weren't pleasant, and I heard the gasps of those who saw the memories. I felt guilty but didn't let up until I had shown them everything I had seen when I was being held in the Warlock's grip, including the slaughter at the Academy, Conrad's forced survival at the hands of the Warlock and his demon followers, and the way the Demon Knight and Wiccan Enforcer had reached for me before the human blood took affect and we were able to kill the Warlock.

When I let go, my head started to pound. I pushed my palms against each side of my skull and said tightly, "It wasn't his fault."

Dara set a hand on my arm. A glance at her showed how much the pushing had taken from her. I lowered my hands. "Thank you," I whispered. She slipped her hand into mine and squeezed it.

"You were under his control, that much is clear, but you chose to let that happen," Briggs argued. His face was pale from what he had seen. "Zanie, the Headmaster, and everyone else would still be alive if it wasn't for you."

Conrad nodded. "That's why I'm here. I want to stop Chutka the Shambler once and for all. I want to end what I started. Then I'll leave and never come back, I promise."

The humility and sorrow in the werewolf's gaze was unmistakable. Even Briggs appeared uncertain as to how to handle Conrad's approach.

"Smell him," I said. "Smell him and tell us if he smells evil. If he does, you're right, we shouldn't trust him; but if not, he deserves a chance to help us end this."

Professor Briggs bowed his head for a moment as if he had been hoping I wouldn't suggest that.

I looked at the Headmistress. She nodded. "That's fair. Trace, will you do it?"

The professor didn't look at me when he walked past. His limp was a brutal reminder of the damage he had barely survived when he attacked Conrad to save my mother. Marks from both werewolf and demon finally made sense. The way that night had impacted Briggs' entire life showed in the heaviness of his steps.

I watched Conrad tense as though he feared Briggs would attack him again. Instead, the professor paused about a foot away.

I heard him sniff. It wasn't tentative or meek. No, the professor wanted to know for himself as much as for the rest of us. He leaned in as he breathed out, then sucked in a breath inches from Conrad's chest. It struck me that the professor smelled the werewolf's heart, the source of life, and the center of what made Conrad who he was.

The professor stepped back with his eyes closed. He sat silently for a few seconds, then let the breath out. He turned away without meeting Conrad's eyes again.

"Well?" the Headmistress demanded.

Professor Briggs glanced at me, then away. He straightened and said, "He smells stained, that's certain, but there is no evil in that man." The admission seemed to take something from him. I couldn't tell if disappointment or anger made the professor's hands clench, but he was quiet for several long seconds before he finally let out a breath and glanced at the Headmistress. "This is your call, Fanny."

Headmistress Wrengold looked around at the students. "The actions we take at this school impact the rest of mythic kind." She hesitated, then said, "We can't punish someone for something beyond their control. As much as I miss my husband, I know you wouldn't do that of your own accord." Her voice lowered and she held Conrad's gaze. "I remember what a good student you were. Rowdy, a bit out of control, perhaps, but good." A single tear fell down her cheek. "You weren't a murderer. And I have wrestled with that thought ever since that night. This may not have been the most conventional way to find out what happened," she said with a glance at me. "But it's right that we learn the truth."

The Headmistress looked at each professor in turn. At last, she held Professor Briggs' gaze until he gave a reluctant, short nod.

"Your assistance is welcome, Conrad Roe. Welcome back," she said. "We have an empty room in the professors' wing you can call your own until this matter is resolved."

Conrad sagged in relief. He grabbed my shoulder and squeezed it. Professor Briggs turned and stalked away through the students without another word. I felt as though I had betrayed him somehow, but I couldn't take it back.

Later that night I was sitting on my bed toying with my cellphone. It wasn't set up for anything but phone calls and texts, yet the last text I had received was the one that warned me of my parents' kidnapping. I couldn't help checking it every few minutes to ensure that they were still safe. It was an unsettling feeling.

I eventually forced myself to put it down and glanced at Alden's bed for the hundredth time. I hadn't seen the Grim since we returned to the Academy. The thought that he and Sparrow might be wandering around somewhere brought me to my feet. I missed the sylph dragon. I wouldn't feel completely at home back at Haunted High without the little black and purple creature either around my wrist near her name or up riding on my shoulder as had become her new favorite place.

I found myself searching for his scent as I climbed the stairs. The thought made me chuckle to myself. Even in human form, I would forever be a werewolf. That thought didn't have the sting it used to; instead, I embraced the other side of me, the side I was still getting to know.

Alden's scent reached my nose. It was fresh. He must have just gone up the stairs. I took them three at a time, anxious to see both of my friends and hope they didn't hold a grudge toward me for leaving them behind.

"Alden, there you are! I've been worried about you," I said when I reached the thirteenth floor and saw the Grim sitting beneath the window at the end.

I crossed the hallway toward him, but slowed when he lifted his head. Tears showed on his cheeks and the anguish on his face was unmistakable.

"I'm so sorry, Finn."

I dropped to my knees in front of him. "Alden, what's wrong?"

He lifted his wrist. It was conspicuously empty.

"Where's Sparrow?" I asked, unable to hide the fear in my voice.

Alden gestured above him. "I brought her up here every day like you asked me to. She hunted for bugs and loved to fly around. She even caught a grasshopper once. I don't know how it got up here, especially at this time of year, and it was disgusting to watch her eat it, but she was so happy and you should have seen how good she slept after that. She even caught—"

"Alden, tell me where she is!" I said, panic making my voice tight.

Alden lowered his light blue eyes from mine. "She's gone, Finn. The other day she flew out the window and hasn't come back."

I stared at the window above him. The glass was open a crack, just wide enough for a baby sylph dragon to slip through.

"No," I said, rising to my feet. I shoved the window up. "No!"

"I don't know how it happened," Alden said. "The window was never open before. I thought maybe somebody went to the clubhouse and she followed them up there, but when I checked it, the clubhouse was empty and Sparrow was nowhere to be found." He buried his face in his hands. "You trusted me and I let you down. I'm so sorry!"

I didn't know what to say or do. On impulse, I climbed out of the window and called for the dragon as I balanced my way to the clubhouse entrance. A quick check inside showed exactly what Alden had said, nothing. I climbed back down and returned to the window. Inside, I could see my friend hunched over with guilt. I glanced around again. Only the city buildings and the washed-out night sky overhead was visible. No dragon was there to answer my call.

I clambered back inside and did my best to calm my expression. I set a hand on Alden's shoulder. "You didn't do anything wrong," I said, willing my voice to remain steady. "It's not your fault. I'm sure she'll come back."

But I wasn't sure. I wasn't sure at all. The dragon had been entrusted to me. She had even sacrificed her life to me and then sworn herself to me instead of going with the Grim to whatever lay beyond for sylph dragons. I had left her in the hopes of keeping her out of danger, but maybe she had felt betrayed. Maybe she had gone off searching for me.

Guilt squeezed my heart so hard it hurt in a way that reminded me of being on Sir Harbrand's table. I took several steadying breaths and the pain slowly faded. Without any other option, I held out my hand to Alden. "I don't blame you. I'm the one who left her. This is on my shoulders, not yours."

The little Grim surprised me by throwing his arms around me and hugging me tight.

"I thought you'd hate me for sure," he said with a sob. "You're my best friend here and pretty much my only friend unless I have food that Brack wants or if I let someone else study from my notes." He stepped back. "I don't know what I'd do if you were mad at me."

"I'm not mad," I said, trying to reassure us both. "We'll figure out how to get her back. I doubt she's gone far."

It took all of my willpower not to run straight to Professor Seedly, shake him out of bed, and demand to know how to find the sylph dragon. Only the fact that she had been gone several days kept me walking to the room I shared with the Grim. It would have to wait until morning.

I settled on my bed and shut my eyes. I could hear Alden sniff occasionally in his bed and felt horrible for the worry I had inadvertently caused him when I entrusted him to watch over Sparrow.

Sparrow was so innocent and young. She was too fragile to be out in the world by herself, especially in a world that didn't believe dragons existed in the first place. But she knew where home was, and I had returned to her before. I hoped that after she had her adventure, she would come back to the place where I always returned. I told myself that everything would work out. It just had to.

On the cliff's edge between sleep and awake, a sound caught my attention. My eyes flew open just as hands grabbed my arms and legs. A black bag was thrown over my head. I struggled to break free.

"Move and die," someone whispered into my ear.

I threw him over my shoulder. Something slammed into my head and everything went dark.

About the Author

Cheree Alsop is an award-winning, best-selling author who has published over 40 books. She is the mother of a beautiful, talented daughter and amazing twin sons who fill every day with joy and laughter. She is married to her best friend, Michael, the light of her life and her soulmate who shares her dreams and inspires her by reading the first drafts and giving much appreciated critiques. Cheree works as a fulltime author and mother, which is more play than work! She enjoys reading, traveling to tropical beaches, riding motorcycles, spending time with her wonderful children, and going on family adventures while planning her next book.

Cheree and Michael live in Utah where they rock out, enjoy the outdoors, plan great quests, and never stop dreaming.

REVIEWS

The Girl from the Stars Series

This is my favorite Cheree Alsop book now! Her best yet! I loved it. So many twists and turns, great characters, excitement and hints of romance. I can't wait for the next one in the series.

—Voca Matisse, Reviewer

Fantastic book! Cheree's ability to write an amazing character that you not only sympathize with but also grow to care for, is one of the fabulous writing abilities that she lends to every story. This story line was full of epic twists and wry humor that had me engaged the entire way through. All in all a fun enjoyable read.

—akgodwin, Amazon Reviewer

This was one of the best books I have read in a while. Sci-fi, adventure, thriller... could not put the book away. I already bought the second book in the series, and hope the third will come out soon.

—Kindle Customer

The main character, Liora, is a very mixed up but emerging person who is a genetic mutt! Half of her DNA is totally violence oriented whilst the other half is straight human, which is to say violent when necessary but basically well rounded. In the beginning she was a slave in a circus and had never known anyone she could trust or care for, and even when she is rescued from that hell she has a hard time adjusting to the idea that she can fit in anywhere. The action is frequent and well written and over time she keeps trying to both find reasons to fit in and reasons to strike out on her own. This is not resolved in the first book, and makes you want to read more. I like the series a lot and hope the writer keeps them coming.

—Sam, Amazon Reviewer

Dr Wolf, the Fae Rift Series

Dr. Wolf, the Fae Rift Series Book 1- Shockwave by Cheree Alsop is a movie transcript ready and suspensefully alluring tale that weaves the mind of the reader around the world of wild dreams.

— Rachel Anderson, Amazon Reviewer

Wow! Was not expecting enjoying this book as much as I did. Ms. Alsop had me drawn in front the get go. The writing was fantastic, the story just flowed so easily and I could not put the book down. I enjoyed all the characters and love her imagination. The banter with the characters had me laughing out loud (I love the fairy and the vampire). I really enjoyed the storyline and the whole what if of falling into a rift. I would highly recommend this book to anyone looking for a nice fresh look on paranormal.

— Amazon Verified Reviewer

Demon Spiral picks up right where Shockwave left off…Once again, I could not put this book down. The flow of the story is amazing and the banter that the author was able to put into the book just made for a very enjoyable read. I highly recommend Cheree Alsop and look forward to reading the next in this series as well.

—Crystal's Review, GoodReads Reviewer

I had to download the sample for this because I was sure I wanted it. I bought the book after the first page. It's almost like Dr. Who with Fae.

—Chris Hughes, Amazon Reviewer

The Silver Series

"Cheree Alsop has written *Silver* for the YA reader who enjoys both werewolves and coming-of-age tales. Although I don't fall into this demographic, I still found it an entertaining read on a long plane trip! The author has put a great deal of thought into balancing a tale that could apply to any teen (death of a parent, new school, trying to find one's place in the world) with the added spice of a youngster dealing with being exceptionally different from those around him, and knowing that puts him in danger."

—Robin Hobb, author of the Farseer Trilogy

"I honestly am amazed this isn't absolutely EVERYWHERE! Amazing book. Could NOT put it down! After reading this book, I purchased the entire series!"

—Josephine, Amazon Reviewer

"A page-turner that kept me wide awake and wanting more. Great characters, well written, tenderly developed, and thrilling. I loved this book, and you will too."

—Valerie McGilvrey

"Super glad that I found this series! I am crushed that it is at its end. I am sure we will see some of the characters in the next series, but it just won't be the same. I am 41 years old, and am only a little embarrassed to say I was crying at 3 a.m. this morning while finishing the last book. Although this is a YA series, all ages will enjoy the Silver Series. Great job by

Cheree Alsop. I am excited to see what she comes up with next."

—Jennc, Amazon Reviewer

The Werewolf Academy Series

If you love werewolves, paranormal, and looking for a book like House of Night or Vampire Academy this is it! YA for sure.

—Reviewer for Sweets Books

I got this book from a giveaway, and it's one of the coolest books I have ever read. If you love Hogwarts, and Vampire Academy, or basically anything that has got to do with supernatural people studying, this is the book for you.

—Maryam Dinzly

This series is truly a work of art, sucked in immediately and permanently. The first line and you are in the book. Cheree Alsop is a gifted writer, all of her books are my complete favorites!! This series has to be my absolute favorite, Alex is truly a wonderful character who I so wish was real so I can meet him and thank him. Once you pick this book up you won't put it down till it's finished. A must read!!!!!

—BookWolf Brianna

Listed with Silver Moon as the top most emotional of Cheree's books, I loved Instinct for its raw truth about the pain, the heartbreak, and the guilt that Alex fights.

—Loren Weaver

Great story. Loaded with adventure at every turn. Can't wait till the next book. Very enjoyable, light reading. I would recommend to all young and old readers.

—Sharon Klein

The Galdoni Series

"This is absolutely one of the best books I have ever read in my life! I loved the characters and their personalities, the storyline and the way it was written. The bravery, courage and sacrifice that Kale showed was amazing and had me scolding myself to get a grip and stop crying! This book had adventure, romance and comedy all rolled into one terrific book I LOVED the lesson in this book, the struggles that the characters had to go through (especially the forbidden love)...I couldn't help wondering what it would be like to live among such strangely beautiful creatures that acted, at times, more caring and compassionate than the humans. Overall, I loved this book...I recommend it to ANYONE who fancies great books."

—iBook Reviewer

"I was not expecting a free novel to beat anything that I have ever laid eyes upon. This book was touching and made me want more after each sentence."

—Sears1994, iBook Reviewer

"This book was simply heart wrenching. It was an amazing book with a great plot. I almost cried several times. All of the scenes were so real it felt like I was there witnessing everything."

—Jeanine Drake, iBook Reveiwer

"Galdoni is an amazing book; it is the first to actually make me cry! It is a book that really touches your heart, a romance novel that might change the way you look at someone. It did that to me."

—Coralee2, Reviewer

"Wow. I simply have no words for this. I highly recommend it to anyone who stumbled across this masterpiece. In other words, READ IT!"

—Troublecat101, iBook Reviewer

The Monster Asylum Series

What a rollercoaster, wow!! I never ever cried when reading a vampire book, but I did this time. I must say it's the best vampire book I've read since ever. One of the best books ever read so far.

—Conny, Goodreads Reviewer

I downloaded this book because of Cheree, I love her imagination. This one is so much fun to read; once I started I couldn't put it down. And now I believe not all Monsters are bad!! Looking forward to the next book in the series. Thanks Cheree

—Doughgirl61, Amazon Reviewer

Keeper of the Wolves

"This is without a doubt the VERY BEST paranormal romance/adventure I have ever read and I've been reading these types of books for over 45 years. Excellent plot, wonderful protagonists—even the evil villains were great. I read this in one sitting on a Saturday morning when there were so many other things I should have been doing. I COULD NOT put it down! I also appreciated the author's research and insights into the behavior of wolf packs. I will CERTAINLY read more by this author and put her on my 'favorites' list."

—N. Darisse

"This is a novel that will emotionally cripple you. Be sure to keep a box of tissues by your side. You will laugh, you will cry, and you will fall in love with Keeper. If you loved *Black Beauty* as a child, then you will truly love *Keeper of the Wolves* as an adult. Put this on your 'must read' list."

—Fortune Ringquist

"Cheree Alsop mastered the mind of a wolf and wrote the most amazing story I've read this year. Once I started, I couldn't stop reading. Personal needs no longer existed. I turned the last page with tears streaming down my face."

—Rachel Andersen, Amazon Reviewer

"I just finished this book. Oh my goodness, did I get emotional in some spots. It was so good. The courage and love portrayed is amazing. I do recommend this book. Thought provoking."

—Candy, Amazon Reviewer

Thief Prince

"I absolutely loved this book! I could not put it down. . . The Thief Prince will whisk you away into a new world that you will not want to leave! I hope that Ms. Alsop has more about this story to write, because I would love more Kit and

Andric! This is one of my favorite books so far this year! Five Stars!"

—Crystal, Book Blogger at Books are Sanity

". . . Once I started I couldn't put it down. The story is amazing. The plot is new and the action never stops. The characters are believable and the emotions presented are beautiful and real. If anyone wants a good, clean, fun, romantic read, look no further. I hope there will be more books set in Debria, or better yet, Antor."

—SH Writer, Amazon Reviewer

"This book was a roller coaster of emotions: tears, laughter, anger, and happiness. I absolutely fell in love with all of the characters placed throughout this story. This author knows how to paint a picture with words."

—Kathleen Vales

"Awesome book! It was so action packed, I could not put it down, and it left me wanting more! It was very well written, leaving me feeling like I had a connection with the characters."

—M. A., Amazon Reviewer

The Shadows Series

"This was a heart-warming tale of rags to riches. It was also wonderfully described and the characters were vivid and vibrant; a story that teaches of love defying boundaries and of people finding acceptance."

—Sara Phillip, Book Reviewer

"This is the best book I have ever had the pleasure of reading. . . It literally has everything, drama, action, fighting, romance, adventure, & suspense. . . Nexa is one of the most incredible female protagonists ever written. . .It literally had me on pins & needles the ENTIRE time. . . I cannot recommend this book highly enough. Please give yourself a wonderful treat & read this book… you will NOT be disappointed!!!"

—Jess- Goodreads Reviewer

"Took my breath away; excitement, adventure and suspense. . . This author has extracted a tender subject and created a supernatural fantasy about seeing beyond the surface of an individual. . . Also the romantic scenes would make a girl swoon. . . The fights between allies and foes and blood lust would attract the male readers. . .The conclusion was so powerful and scary this reader was sitting on the edge of her seat."

—Susan Mahoney, Book Blogger

"Adventure, incredible amounts of imagination and description go into this world! It is a buy now, don't leave the couch until the last chapter has reached an end kind of read!"

—Malcay- Amazon Reviewer

"The high action tale with the underlying love story that unfolds makes you want to keep reading and not put it down. I can't wait until the next book in the Shadows Series comes out."

—Karen- Amazon Reviewer

". . . It's refreshing to see a female character portrayed without the girly clichés most writers fall into. She is someone I would like to meet in real life, and it is nice to read the first person POV of a character who is so well-round that she is brave, but still has the softer feminine side that defines her character. A definite must read."

—S. Teppen- Goodreads Reviewer

The Small Town Superhero Series

"A very human superhero- Cheree Alsop has written a great book for youth and adults alike. Kelson, the superhero, is battling his own demons plus bullies in this action packed narrative. Small Town Superhero had me from the first sentence through the end. I felt every sorrow, every pain and the delight of rushing through the dark on a motorcycle. Descriptions in Small Town Superhero are so well written the reader is immersed in the town and lives of its inhabitants."

—Rachel Andersen, Book Reviewer

"Anyone who grew up in a small town or around motorcycles will love this! It has great characters and flows well with martial arts fighting and conflicts involved."

—Karen, Amazon Reviewer

"Fantastic story...and I love motorcycles and heroes who don't like the limelight. Excellent character development. You'll like this series!"

—Michael, Amazon Reviewer

"Another great read; couldn't put it down. Would definitely recommend this book to friends and family. She has put out another great read. Looking forward to reading more!"

—Benton Garrison, Amazon Reviewer

"I enjoyed this book a lot. Good teen reading. Most books I read are adult contemporary; I needed a change and this was a good change. I do recommend reading this book! I will be looking out for more books from this author. Thank you!"

—Cass, Amazon Reviewer

Stolen

"This book will take your heart, make it a little bit bigger, and then fill it with love. I would recommend this book to anyone from 10-100. To put this book in words is like trying to describe love. I had just gotten it and I finished it the next day because I couldn't put it down. If you like action, thrilling fights, and/or romance, then this is the perfect book for you."

—Steven L. Jagerhorn

"Couldn't put this one down! Love Cheree's ability to create totally relatable characters and a story told so fluidly you actually believe it's real."

—Sue McMillin, Amazon Reviewer

"I enjoyed this book it was exciting and kept you interested. The characters were believable. And the teen romance was cute."

—Book Haven- Amazon Reviewer

"I really liked this book . . . I was pleasantly surprised to discover this well-written book. . .I'm looking forward to reading more from this author."

—Julie M. Peterson- Amazon Reviewer

"Great book! I enjoyed this book very much it keeps you wanting to know more! I couldn't put it down! Great read!"

—Meghan- Amazon Reviewer

"A great read with believable characters that hook you instantly. . . I was left wanting to read more when the book was finished."

—Katie- Goodreads Reviewer

Heart of the Wolf

"Absolutely breathtaking! This book is a roller coaster of emotions that will leave you exhausted!!! A beautiful fantasy filled with action and love. I recommend this book to all fantasy lovers and those who enjoy a heartbreaking love story that rivals that of Romeo and Juliet. I couldn't put this book down!"

—Amy May

"What an awesome book! A continual adventure, with surprises on every page. What a gifted author she is. You just can't put the book down. I read it in two days. Cheree has a way of developing relationships and pulling at your heart. You find yourself identifying with the characters in her book...True life situations make this book come alive for you and gives you increased understanding of your own situation in life. Magnificent story and characters. I've read all of Cheree's books and recommend them all to you...especially if you love adventures."

—Michael, Amazon Reviewer

"You'll like this one and want to start part two as soon as you can! If you are in the mood for an adventure book in a faraway kingdom where there are rival kingdoms plotting and scheming to gain more power, you'll enjoy this novel. The characters are well developed, and of course with Cheree there is always a unique supernatural twist thrown into the story as well as romantic interests to make the pages fly by."

Karen, Amazon Reviewer

When Death Loved an Angel

"This style of book is quite a change for this author so I wasn't expecting this, but I found an interesting story of two very different souls who stepped outside of their "accepted roles" to find love and forgiveness, and what is truly of value in life and death."

—Karen, Amazon Reviewer

"When Death Loved an Angel by Cheree Alsop is a touching paranormal romance that cranks the readers' thinking mode into high gear."

—Rachel Andersen, Book Reviewer

"Loved this book. I would recommend this book to everyone. And be sure to check out the rest of her books, too!"

—Malcay, Book Reviewer

The Million Dollar Gift

...This was a very beautiful, heart warming story about a young man who finds love, and family again on Christmas. I really enjoyed this short story. It truly inspires the meaning of

Christmas in my eyes. It was utterly beautiful, and I highly recommend it. The plot is very interesting, and the characters catch your heart and lead on this very sad and happy story.

—Whitney@Shooting Stars Review

I recommend The Million Dollar Gift as a way to remember what Christmas is about: Love. Family. Friendship. Because a life without love isn't really worth living anyway.

—Loren Weaver

When Chase risks his life to save a brother and sister just before Christmas, his life becomes entwined with theirs more intricately than he could have imagined. Emotional and moving, this is a story of a young man whose troubled heart is tested by the one thing he is unprepared to face, love. MY TAKE- This is a fast, fun, emotional Christmas read. Made me cry.

—Donna Weaver

Never stop dreaming!

Printed in Great Britain
by Amazon

45289626R00135